FORGOTTEN
RIDER JACOBS

Dreamspinner Press

Published by
Dreamspinner Press
5032 Capital Circle SW
Suite 2, PMB# 279
Tallahassee, FL 32305-7886
USA
http://www.dreamspinnerpress.com/

This is a work of fiction. Names, characters, places, and incidents either are the product of author imagination or are used fictitiously, and any resemblance to actual persons, living or dead, business establishments, events, or locales is entirely coincidental.

Cover Art
© 2014 Christine Griffin.
alizarin_griffin@yahoo.com
http://christinegriffin.artworkfolio.com/
Cover content is for illustrative purposes only and any person depicted on the cover is a model.

ISBN: 978-1-62798-430-0
Digital ISBN: 978-1-62798-429-4

Printed in the United States of America
First Edition
March 2014

For my parents, who encouraged me to read and write and instilled a love for things that go bump in the night.

For Angel, who was my sounding board. I will always and forever miss you.

For Johanna, Mindy, and David, who are always ready for the book to come out and asking me for more.

Prologue

August 2010

SARA AWOKE with a start. The soft sounds of muffled crying filled the bedroom. She snuggled further under the blanket, as if that would keep the noise at bay. The sobs rose in crescendo, the soft weeping becoming a wail of pain. She pressed the pillow over her head, hoping that would block out the cries, but they penetrated the plump pillow almost as if she had nothing over her ears.

Light footsteps hurried down the hallway toward the bathroom, and then the door slammed shut. Sara steeled her nerves and crawled out of bed. She reached on the floor and grabbed the clothes she had worn earlier. If she was going to flee the house, she refused to do it in her nightgown. She dressed as quickly as she could, listening to heavy footfalls of a second person walking toward the bathroom.

Sara began to tiptoe toward the door, then froze when she heard distinct voices on the other side. Her heart beat loud and hard as she looked around for a place to hide but found nothing that seemed good enough. She hurried back to the side of the bed, slid down the wall, and hid in the shadows that the bed and nightstand provided. If she stayed still enough and small enough, then whoever was in the hallway would never see her wedged there. Doors began to slam, each bang increasing in volume until even the windows rattled under the force.

Sara huddled in the space between the bed and the wall, trying to make herself as small as possible. Her eyes were glued to the bedroom door, and her breath came out in short bursts as if even the sound of her breathing would alert whatever was in the hall.

She could see her phone sitting on the nightstand on the other side of the bed. It seemed so far away. Carefully she rose—her movements slow to prevent noise. She placed one hand on the side of the bed as she eased herself onto it. The light footfall of someone running barefoot echoed through the house, followed by the much heavier steps of a booted man.

Sara grabbed her phone and scrambled back to her hiding place. Her fingers trembled so badly she dialed the wrong number twice. A shrill scream pierced the night. Sara clamped her hand over her mouth to keep from screaming herself. She heard glass breaking as something was thrown against a wall.

"Hello?"

"Charles," she sobbed into the phone.

"Sara, what's wrong?"

"I don't care what you say or think, but this house is haunted. I won't stay here a moment longer, Charles. You can call up the landlord and tell them we are moving out."

"Sara, calm down. I can't understand what you're saying."

The sound of something solid slamming into the wall came from the room directly below. It hit hard enough to make the wall shake slightly.

"Sara…." Charles sighed into the phone. "There's nothing in the house. The last time I left work, it was tree branch hitting the side of the house."

"It's not a fucking tree branch!" she hissed with as much force as her fear of being heard would allow. "I'm telling you right now, if you don't get here in the next five minutes, I'm walking to the next town. Don't bother to come find me when I do."

"Even if I left right now, which I can't, I wouldn't be there in five minutes." Charles spoke calmly.

The running started again, the slapping of bare feet hitting wooden steps as they ran back up. The heavy steps followed close behind. These steps were slower, unhurried, almost as if they knew there was nowhere in the house to hide. The running came down the hallway, closer to the bedroom door. Sara lifted the edge of the bedspread and tried to decide if she could wiggle her way under the bed.

"Sara?"

"There are people in this house, Charles! They are in the hallway."

"Are you sure? Look, hang up and I'll call the police. They will have a cruiser out there in five, maybe ten minutes tops."

Sara's eyes were glued to the doorknob. A beam of moonlight shone upon the door, illuminating the knob like it was in the middle of a spotlight. It was slowly turning.

"Hang up, Sara, I'll call the police."

The door flew open with enough force that plaster fell as it hit the wall. Sara shrieked, dropping the phone. The back flew off, and the battery skittered under the bed. Something landed on the bed, but Sara saw nothing. A loud scream pieced the night. Sara covered her ears to try and block it out. Above her, a shadow loomed, twisting and pulsing as if alive.

Sara scrambled on her hands and knees from her hiding place. She stumbled to her feet and ran from the room. Behind her, the bedroom door slammed shut. Sara ran down the hall as the bedroom door once again flew open. A wind as strong and violent as a tornado rushed past her, knocking her off her feet and the pictures from the wall.

"*Get out of my house!*" the voice cried out.

Sara climbed to her feet. Grabbing the stair railing to keep from falling, she hurried down the stairs, willing her feet to go faster but feeling as if her movements were in slow motion. The cold wind blew through Sara and knocked her down the last few steps.

She lay on the floor for a moment, stunned and breathless. A large black shadow loomed over her. She rolled over, struggling to her feet, a sharp pain shooting through her ankle. Nothing would keep her in the house a moment longer. The shadow stood between her and the front door.

"I want to live!" The voice screamed again.

Sara limped to the french doors. As she yanked them open, a coffee table hit the wall on her left. The sound of the larger furniture moving propelled her forward, the pain in her ankle all but forgotten.

Sara hurried onto the porch, but the fury was just as bad outside. The porch swing they had installed just a few weeks before rocked back and forth, bumping into the house. The trees bent low in the wind, but the stars shone brightly above in the cloudless sky. Sara stumbled off the porch and into the yard. A trash can sailed past her head, landed in the yard, and bounced into the nearest tree.

Wanting to be as far away from the house as possible, Sara rushed across the yard. As she glanced over her shoulder, the curtain in the front room was pulled back. She was sure she could see a man standing there in the window before the curtain fell back in place. She ran from the house. The fury abated the farther away she got. Finally on the gravel road, she bent over and rested her hands on her knees as she gasped, trying to catch her breath. From here, the house looked peaceful, almost tranquil.

She turned and walked down the road. She would have someone else pack up her things. She didn't care what it cost to get them out here in nowhere town, but she was never setting foot in that house again.

Chapter 1

September 2013

"RHYS, WE don't need a house this big," Peter protested as they walked through the empty house, looking at each of the rooms and imagining the potential. Peter saw nothing more than outdated wallpaper, scratched wooden floors, and dust everywhere.

"It's perfect," Rhys breathed, looking up at the vaulted ceilings and crown molding. He ran his fingers over one of the frosted-glass windows embedded in the front door. Rhys loved old homes, claiming they had character that new prefabbed homes didn't.

"It's five bedrooms," Peter countered as Rhys touched the wood of the windowsill. His protest was probably a waste of breath. "It's a farm. What are we going to do with all this land? Hell, I think a third is woods, and the rest is so overgrown it'll take years to cut it all back."

"Look at these hardwood floors." Rhys knelt to inspect the dirty boards. "All we have to do is give them a good buffing, and they'll be like new."

Peter wiped the sweat from his brow. The day had grown unusually hot and humid for September. "I know they're nice floors. I love the floors. You know how I feel about hardwood floors, but beautiful floors are not a reason to buy a house."

"I wonder what kind of wood they used. It looks like two different colors," Rhys murmured as he crawled across the floor.

"The floors were replaced in the late 1930s when an art dealer purchased the home," the real estate agent informed them. "He did a lot of renovations, making things modern—at least until he became too old to do so. In the last couple of years, the various occupants have added their own personal touches here and there—marble countertops in the kitchen, new cabinets in the bathroom, and such. We had a house inspection done before we put it on market. I can assure you the electrical and plumbing all meet code."

"This house will take a lot of work." Peter knew the house had sat empty for the last year, and it looked like it. Before that, the house would rent out for six months, maybe a year, before the renters would pack up and flee in the night. Okay maybe *flee* was a bit harsh, but he was a writer, and he could picture the renters running from the house in terror.

"It won't take that much work. We can get a buffer to clean up the floor, put some paint on the walls, and we're good." Rhys stood. Dusting his hands off on his jeans, he turned to Peter and gave him his sexiest smile.

Peter walked to the middle of the room, his footsteps echoing on the wooden floor. He slowly turned in a circle, taking in the whole front room. The floors were dirty, the wallpaper peeling, and in a few places the plaster had fallen. It would take more than a mop and a coat of paint.

Peter touched the wall, feeling the rough texture of the wallpaper. It would all have to come off. He wished he could count on Rhys to help him, but the man had the attention span of a gnat. Peter walked toward the sweeping staircase—something he loved, not that he would tell Rhys that, at least not yet. The moment he mentioned he liked something, Rhys grabbed hold of the fact like a bulldog, refusing to let it go. Peter stared up the stairs. For the briefest of moments, he thought he saw a shadow move across the wall. Tilting his head to one side, forehead wrinkled in confusion, he placed his foot on the first step, intending to find out exactly what he thought he'd seen.

"The house was built in the 1840s. Much of the wood is original. It does need some TLC, but with the right owner, this house could easily double in price."

"I admit the price is good, almost too good, if you ask me." Peter had to agree, turning away from the stairs. "I'm just afraid we'll sink a small fortune to bring it up to the twenty-first century. So why has the house never been for sale until now?"

"Well, the owner, Demetri Romanov, refused to sell it. When he became too old to care for the house, he was moved into a nursing home and the house sat empty. The city asked several times if he would consider selling it, but he refused to do so.

"Demetri appointed power of attorney to Mr. Randolph Kramer in 1985. He made Mr. Kramer promise to never sell the house. He did go against Demetri's wishes and rented it out. I don't know if it was just too much house for the renters or what, but no one ever stayed more than six months."

"So why sell it now?" Peter asked, curiosity getting the better of him.

"Mr. Kramer has only been to the house a half-dozen times since Mr. Romanov died in '92. He has grown tired of the expense of keeping a house this large, and since no one stays in it, he has decided to sell. I can tell you, he is very motivated."

"Why does no one stay?" Rhys asked. "Is it haunted or something?"

The agent laughed. "How funny. Are you the writer?"

"No, that would be me." Peter smiled. "He has a point, though. Is there a reason no one stays in the house?"

She shrugged. "No one ever says. I honestly just think it is the size of the house and the land that goes with it. The price may be good, but three hundred acres is a lot of land to take care of. It has some wonderful pastoral land, but with the drought, many people had to sell off their cows, and it isn't economical to own a family farm anymore."

Peter watched Rhys walk off toward one of the other rooms as he tried to think of more questions. "I really don't see us farming. I guess I just worry about the things you find out after you move in, like the basement has a giant sinkhole."

Rhys walked back to Peter. He slid his hand up and down Peter's broad chest, a small smile on his lips. "You're way too overdramatic. Just think about the possibilities. We can both have an office in this house. You said it would be better if we had our own space. That's the reason we're looking for a house to start with."

"I thought perhaps three bedrooms and an office. You could convert one of the bedrooms, and I'd have the office. I want something small and more personal, not a five-bedroom, three-story farmhouse with three hundred plus acres," Peter countered.

"We can get so much more house for the same price we'd pay in the city. I say we take it."

Peter gave a soft sigh of defeat. He could never tell Rhys no.

"I can't help it, Peter. This house speaks to me. I know this is where we're supposed to be."

"I guess if you're sure about this...." There was no point in arguing with Rhys once he set his heart on something.

Rhys nodded as he headed for the french doors that led onto the porch. "I'm more than sure about this. We are getting in each other's way back in the city. The office has become too small for either of us, the city too loud and crazy."

Rhys walked out the side door and onto the wraparound porch. Peter looked around the empty room once again, unable to shake the feeling he wasn't alone. He imagined an anticipation of sound, as though any moment he'd hear a voice or a burst of laughter. He strained to hear it, expected it, even though he knew they were alone. They had been all over the house, and other than Rhys and the agent, no one else was there.

Rhys stood on the porch, staring at the small orchard in the distance.

"It smells like fall out here," Peter stated from the doorway.

"You're right about the size of the house. The porch wraps halfway around the house. It has a widow's walk on top, and the attic has been finished so it could be used as either an office or another bedroom. The walls need paint, the yard will require a lot of work...." Rhys let the thought trail off for a moment. "I know you need quiet places to meditate and think through your story ideas. You can convert one of the bedrooms into an office, and I'll turn the attic into my space. The large open attic is enough for me to move around, to try out the moves before I program them in. We can be on separate floors so we won't bother each other like we are in the apartment," Rhys stated, as Peter crossed the porch. "It seems like every time one of us tries to work, the other is already in there. You have to write in the front room because my game design storyboard takes up more space than your computer, but even then, anytime we watch TV, you have to pick up everything. We won't trip over each other here. This house has everything I want, everything we need. I think we should get the house, Peter."

Peter wrapped his arms around Rhys's slim waist and rested his head against his back. "You know I love you?"

Rhys reached down to take Peter's hand. "More than anything, right?"

Peter placed a gentle kiss between his shoulder blades. "More than anything."

"If you really think we can't afford it…." Rhys sighed, rubbing the arm that held his waist as he stared at the tree line.

Peter shook his head, a smile on his lips. "I worry, you know that. You see potential. I see bills. You see large open rooms. I think about heating the place. You did say we needed to get away from the distractions of the city. I wasn't aware getting away from it all meant a farmhouse two hours away."

"If I truly thought we couldn't afford the upkeep, I wouldn't want it so much. You did well last year. Three of your books will have sequels out this year. My job is secure. I work from home. The last video game I designed became a megasuccess. We can afford it, Peter."

"You work too hard, you know that?" Peter brushed an imaginary piece of lint from Rhys's shoulder.

"Me? You're the one who has to continue writing three different series. I just have to play a video game." Rhys laughed, and for a moment Peter's world was right.

"I love what I do, you know that. I have all these stories tumbling around in my head waiting to get out. I have an exciting job. You, on the other hand…."

"My job is exciting too." Rhys pouted.

Peter grabbed Rhys's lower lip between his teeth and sucked on the soft skin. Rhys stepped closer, turning the love nip into a deeper kiss.

"Just think, there's all that land for you to explore, to take pictures of. It'll change with the seasons, and you won't have to go far for inspiration. You need your camera to inspire you, to bring places in your books to life," he pointed out as Peter stepped away.

Peter walked slowly along the porch, trailing his hand along the railing, feeling the rough wood under his fingers as he thought about what Rhys had said. He would have to replace a few pieces, sand a couple of places, and add a wood sealant. Otherwise the aged boards appeared strong and sturdy. "If I wanted to, I could use the land for several different books. Think of the trees when the snow has just fallen. I can go out at night, get great pictures of the moon over the field, through the trees, shimmering off the pond. I'm starting a new book series, one where I plan to cross cavemen and werewolves, something primitive and ancient, and this area will be great for that. Can't you see the wolves among the trees? What about my Western series? The open space down by the pond would be great. I can picture a wagon train crossing it, a family carving out a farm."

Rhys chuckled. "Are you trying to convince yourself or me?"

Peter sighed, looking out over the yard. He should tell Rhys no. Logically, he knew that. He glanced back at Rhys, whose dark-blue eyes shone with excitement. He had been in Peter's life for the last eight years and had never asked anything from him. Well, nothing this big anyway. The truth was, they could afford the house. It had been reduced dramatically in price.

"A little of both, I guess."

Rhys nodded, turning to sit on the railing. He stared through the double doors into the empty living room. The agent was walking around inside, giving them a little space to discuss the house but trying to overhear all the same.

"I could tell you about the ideas this house would create in your demented mind. There would be stories of vampires and ghosts, of the romantic South…." He trailed off.

"Yeah, I have ideas all right. A desolate house two naive city boys move into, which is actually the home of inbred psychopath killers? I always wanted to branch out into horror," Peter said sarcastically.

Rhys laughed out loud. "You have that wrong. It's a mass of murdering farmers who will sacrifice us to save the crops."

"You really want this house, don't you?" Peter knew the answer before Rhys spoke.

"I really want this house, Peter, to decorate it and make it mine. I've never had a house to call my own. It's always been apartments or duplexes, places we rented, even when I was a child."

Peter gave a deep sigh and leaned against the railing. Rhys was looking at the porch, his toe running back and forth along the peeling paint. He was biting his lip in a way that tugged at Peter's heart. Rhys was expecting Peter to say no. Peter could tell by the way his shoulders were rounded, almost as if he was pulling in on himself, preparing for disappointment. A gentle breeze blew, ruffling Peter's hair. It brought the faintest smells of the country—clean air, traces of the apples that had fallen to the ground. Maybe they could make it work. He did need to start on those books, and decorating the rooms would keep Rhys occupied. He chuckled at the thought. That would keep Rhys occupied for a day, two at the most. Rhys was brilliant, creative, could program a video game for hours, but everything else bored him within minutes.

Rhys wanted the house, and Peter wanted to give the man everything he desired. Still, the upkeep of such a large house would take a lot of time and money.

"Do you think we could get someone out here to do yard work?" Peter asked the agent as she stepped out onto the porch, as if sensing they had reached a decision.

"I'm sure if you advertised at the college, you would find someone willing to do it for a reasonable price."

Peter nodded, casting one last glance at Rhys, who was chewing on his thumbnail and staring expectantly at him. "Submit an offer for $198,000."

"Great. Give me a couple of days, and I'll have the paperwork all drawn up."

Rhys bounced up and down, a smile larger than Peter had ever seen on his face. "This will be our dream house. It'll be everything we wanted and more."

Peter looked back in the house, the feeling he wasn't alone still tingling along his skin. "I hope so, Rhys. I really hope so."

Chapter 2

"WHAT DO you think about this color?" Rhys held a paint swatch against the wall.

Peter stopped polishing the wood trim. Rhys had been right. A lot of elbow grease and the wood shone almost like new. The scratches were shallow, nothing that couldn't be easily fixed. Peter wiped the sweat from his forehead and looked at Rhys. Tilting his head to one side, he tried to picture how the drab sickly-green color would look if it covered all the walls. "I'm not loving it."

Rhys smiled, then pulled a second color out of the bundle he had collected over the last few days. "This is a dove gray. What about it?"

Peter nodded. "Much better. I think it'll be perfect with the black leather furniture we ordered."

"We could have just brought our old stuff," Rhys pointed out, sifting through the colors he still held in his hand.

Peter shook his head. After putting a little more polish on his rag, he bent down to continue wiping the baseboards. "A new house deserves new furniture. We've left the old apartment life behind and are actually homeowners."

Rhys held up a third color. "I liked the furniture we had. It had many good memories attached to it. I think we'll do the trim in green."

"Like hell we will. I didn't spend the last five hours buffing out scratches and polishing wood to have you paint over it." Peter tossed the rag on the floor as he sat back. He wiped a drop of sweat from his cheek, leaving a streak of dirt. He leaned forward a little and rested his arms on his knees. "You're right, about the furniture. I think we were creating one of those memories when we broke the dining room chair."

Rhys sighed, dropping the paint swatches on the floor. "Let's take a break from choosing colors and grab a bite to eat."

"Pizza?" Peter asked. He brought the long slim fingers to his lips for a kiss.

"Actually, I was thinking this would be the perfect time to break in the front room." Rhys knelt before him and shuffled forward until he was between Peter's legs.

"Pizza first, you for dessert." Peter smiled, turning Rhys's hand over so he could place a gentle kiss on his palm.

Rhys shook his head, an exaggerated hurt look on his face. "I guess the honeymoon is over, isn't it? It took eight years, but you would rather have food than me."

"Never, darling, but you moved us to the boondocks and things aren't open twenty-four hours like they are in the city. If we want to grab a bite to eat, we need to do it before the pizza place closes." He kissed Rhys's inner wrist.

"If you want, I can run to town and grab a pizza while you work," Rhys offered, closing his eyes.

"I don't know how I can contain my excitement at that thought— you running around town having fun, while I stay here making this rundown shell of a house our home." The hair on the back of Peter's neck stood up. He glanced over his shoulder, the feeling of being watched making him tingle.

"What, sweetie?" Rhys asked, trying to see what had caught Peter's attention.

"Nothing. I just thought I heard something." He turned his attention back to Rhys, who knelt between his legs.

"It was probably just the house settling or something like that. Neither of us has lived in a detached house. Hell, we haven't lived in a house this old either. I'm sure there will be a lot of sounds we will have to find explanations for." Rhys wrapped his arms around Peter's shoulders, his forehead resting against Peter's.

"If I stay here, I can get a few things unpacked," Peter mused. "On the other hand, I want to go with you."

"If you're going with me, you have to stay in the car." Rhys wrinkled his nose. "You are covered with dirt and smell."

Peter tilted his head to one side, trying to see around Rhys.

"What, Peter?" he asked, standing up and offering his hand to help Peter off the floor.

"Nothing. I thought I saw something outside. Remind me to buy some curtains to put over the glass doors. I know there's nothing out there, but I feel like I'm being watched."

Rhys kissed his nose. "Nothing out there but the wildlife."

Peter walked toward the double doors, trying to peer into the inky night. He stared past his own reflection in the glass to see what was out there, what was making his skin tingle, the goose bumps rise, the hair on the back of his neck stand up. He moved closer to the door, squinting. He saw Rhys's reflection in the glass, his white-blond hair hanging over one eye, lips pursed, and arms across his chest. On Rhys's left side stood the staircase. Peter saw something in the reflection, a dark shadow out of place. He focused on the shadow and refused to breathe, as if that would make whatever he was seeing come in a little clearer. The shadow began to form into the vague shape of a man.

"Fuck!" Peter yelled as something overhead slammed shut.

Rhys looked toward the stairs. "What was that? Did you leave a window open, Peter?"

Peter shook his head, his hand on his chest, trying to calm his breathing. "The wind is blowing. It was probably a shutter."

"It almost gave you a heart attack. I don't know what scared me more, the bang upstairs or your scream." Rhys pulled his keys out of his pocket. "Remind me to pick up some hooks so we can fasten the shutters, all right?"

"I didn't scream. I yelled. There is a big difference," Peter countered as he walked toward the stairs. "We should probably head upstairs to check."

15

"I'm hungry, Peter. It was a shutter banging in the wind. Let's go get something to eat."

Peter stopped at the bottom of the stairs. It seemed as though the top steps disappeared into a darkness no light could penetrate. "We need to get a nightlight for the landing too."

"You run up and check." Rhys flipped through the phone book. "I'm going to call in the pizza order."

"Okay, babe. I'll take a quick look around." He glanced at Rhys, who was punching the numbers for the local pizza place.

As Peter walked slowly up the stairs, his feet felt like they were made of lead. He didn't want to go, he didn't want to know what was up there, and he wasn't sure why. The hair on his arms began to stand up. A tremor skittered along his flesh the closer he got to the top of the stairs. Rhys depended on him to be the strong one, though. He had to do this. He had no idea what it was about this house that caused him to be afraid. Maybe Rhys was right—they were city boys. They needed to get someone out here who could put a light switch at the bottom of the stairs. Who only had a light switch at the top?

He counted each step in his head and tried to figure out how he would use them in one of his stories. Maybe the main character would fall down the stairs, tragically dying on his wedding day. Perhaps he would be a turn-of-the-century landowner shot by rival cattle barons, only to make it up to the twelfth step before dying in the arms of his lover.

He ran his hand along the wall, feeling the wood paneling under his fingers as he reached for the light switch. He would pull that paneling down the moment he got a chance.

On the landing, he flipped the switch and bathed the hall in a warm glow. They needed to buy brighter lightbulbs too. The energy savers were nice, but he wanted the hallway lit up at night. At the first door, he stopped and opened it a crack, then slipped his hand in to turn on the light before he opened the door the rest of the way. The room was empty, the bare window closed tight. The next trip into town, they really needed to purchase curtains. Peter had been raised by a mother who kept the curtains closed so the neighbors couldn't see in. It bothered him that almost anyone—should anyone be this far out in the country—could see inside his house. The voice of his mother echoing in his head was probably what caused him to feel such unease.

"Are you ready to go?" Rhys called up.

"Yeah," Peter replied, crossing the room. He glanced back over his shoulder one last time. He saw no reason to check the rest of the rooms for the loose shutter.

"Find the shutter?" Rhys asked as Peter appeared.

"I wasn't sure which one it was. I'll tighten them all tomorrow."

Rhys tossed Peter the keys as he jogged down the stairs. "You're driving."

"You got the pizza ordered?" Peter caught the keys as he walked across the front room heading for the back door.

Rhys nodded, following close behind. "Bacon, olives, onions, and banana peppers, with mushrooms on half. I made sure it was thin crust, just the way you like it. She said it should be ready in twenty minutes."

Peter pulled the back door shut, locking it as he did. He knew in theory no one in the country locked their doors, but old habits died hard. Peter glanced over his shoulder at the house as he stepped off the porch and headed for the car. Noticing they'd left the front room light on, he stopped for a moment as the light from the window was blocked, almost as if someone stood in front of it.

"Get in the car, Peter." Rhys opened the passenger-side door. "I left a few lights on so it wouldn't be so dark when we got home."

Peter looked back, but the shadow was no longer in front of the window. He shook his head, climbed into the car, pulled out of the driveway, and headed into town.

Chapter 3

"WATCHING YOU undress is so sexy." Peter leaned back against the headboard.

Rhys tossed his shirt in Peter's direction. "I'm getting undressed for bed, nothing sexy about that. You've seen me undress how many times over the last eight years?"

"Sometimes I find the simplest things can be the most erotic."

"Only when you're horny," Rhys commented dryly as he unzipped his pants. He had to wiggle his hips a little to get them down.

"Not always," Peter argued, fluffing his pillows before sliding down under the covers.

"No, you're not always horny. So what did you do?" Rhys picked his jeans up off the floor.

"Give the man a compliment and he tries to read something into it." Peter tried to sound wounded. He rolled his eyes, giving a slight shake of his head as he watched Rhys put up his dirty clothes. It was one of the odd quirks that he loved about the man. Peter let his gaze trail over Rhys's body. His hair was dyed a white blond. Peter didn't think he had ever seen Rhys's natural hair color. Well, that wasn't true. He had seen Rhys's school pictures once. The child with dark-blond hair and missing front teeth had smiled at the camera with the same infectious smile he still had. The tapered haircut from Rhys's youth had changed to a skater boy cut in his teens and then to the sharp-edged cuts of an anime character as he grew into adulthood. It was much the same style he now had, the cut changing but still looking like something found in a manga.

Rhys was tall but small boned. The closest he came to working out was in his video games. The rail-thin body of his youth had turned into the heavier body of a man, much of the weight settling around his middle, giving him the cutest love handles. Rhys hated gaining weight, positive it all settled in his waist and thighs, but Peter loved him all the more. They had both gained weight over the last eight years, and each change Rhys's body went through, every laugh line and wrinkle, made Peter love him just a little more.

Rhys crawled across the bed until he was by Peter's side. "I'm just being honest, sweetie. We've been married for several years now. I know all your tricks."

"Kiss?" Peter asked, tilting his head back.

Rhys kissed the tip of Peter's nose before he slid under the covers. He snuggled close, his arm going across Peter's chest. "I think we'll get the kitchen unpacked next. I feel better when my kitchen is stocked and in order, then I think we should polish all the wood in the front room once more, and it will be done."

"Do you know how many times I've polished the wood? You had me buff out the scratches, use wood oil to rehydrate it, like it needed that, and then you had me wipe it down twice." Peter whined a little. "You do know how much wood is in that room?"

Rhys kissed his neck. "I know how much wood is in the front room. One last time, and I'll be happy. We have the room painted. We have the furniture sitting in the middle of it. Clean the wood and buff the floors one more time, and I swear we can call that room done."

"Then we start on which room?" Peter asked, sliding his fingers though Rhys's hair as Rhys placed his head on Peter's shoulder.

"I think the dining room. It won't take much. We can paint the walls a nice cherry color to go with the cherry wood table, accent it in cream since the wood in there is already painted white. Clean the dust off the chandelier, and that's it. We'll be done in no time. I want that room to be classically simple."

"I'm not sure cherry is the proper color for a dining room." Peter ran the tip of his finger along Rhys's firm jaw, feeling the slight stubble of the day's growth.

"Cherry is the perfect color. It's the color I want," Rhys argued, tilting his head toward Peter's hand.

Peter gave a soft sigh of defeat as he brushed his thumb over Rhys's lower lip. Rhys nipped at the digit, a smile on his face. "You know the only way you will be happy is if I'm happy."

Peter chuckled as he kissed the top of Rhys's head. "If it makes you happy, I'll do the wood one more time."

Rhys pulled the blankets up, under his chin. He rubbed his cheek against Peter's chest. "Thank you, lover."

"Any chance I'll get lucky?" Peter asked, tightening his grip on Rhys's waist.

"Nope."

Peter reached down, pulling Rhys's leg higher until it covered his crotch. He rubbed Rhys's thigh, wiggling his hip against Rhys's cock.

"Feeling your erection pressed against my leg doesn't mean I'm going to change my mind," Rhys murmured sleepily, sliding his leg down until it was in a much more comfortable position.

"You should be happy that after eight years, I still get an erection when I see you undress."

"Still not going to put out for you." Rhys rolled over so his back was to Peter and scooted back until he was pressed against him.

"You've always needed to touch me in order to sleep. It makes me wonder how you survived those long, lonely twenty-three years without me." Peter rolled onto his side so they could spoon. It had been hard for him when they'd first started sleeping together. Peter hadn't been used to a man who needed his touch, who curled up against his chest to sleep. Now, though, he couldn't imagine sleeping without Rhys pressed firmly against him.

"It was hard, but with the help of a body pillow I managed to survive." He squirmed a little, trying to get more comfortable, pressing his ass firmly against Peter's hips.

Peter kissed the back of Rhys's neck, running his hand up and down his chest. "How about heavy petting?"

Rhys wasn't able to stop the slight shudder that ran through him as Peter licked his neck. "No heavy petting, Peter. Go to sleep."

Peter gave a soft sigh, his breath ruffling Rhys's hair. "So much for breaking in every room in the house."

Rhys took Peter's hand and brought it up until it was over his heart. "I love you, baby, I really do. I just don't remember telling you we would break in every room in one night. I'm tired. We worked hard, harder than this little gamer is used to. Now snuggle me close and kiss me goodnight."

"How about this, if I rub little Rhys and he responds, can we have sex?" Peter slid his hand to the front of Rhys's boxers.

"I think if you value your fingers, you better raise them up about six inches," Rhys responded, pulling the hand back up until it rested on his stomach. "Now go to sleep."

Peter placed small kisses along the back of Rhys's neck and across his shoulder before rubbing his cheek against the smooth skin. "I love you too, baby. Pleasant dreams."

"Pleasant dreams, sweetie." He sighed softly, feeling Rhys snuggle down behind him.

Peter closed his eyes, and it wasn't long before Rhys's breathing became deep and steady. He snuggled just a little, pulling the man to him before he also drifted off to sleep.

Peter walked slowly though the front room, and felt glad to see it finally in order. He had begun to worry that Rhys would never declare the room done enough that the furniture could be placed somewhere other than a heap in the middle. He vaguely wondered when Rhys had moved everything; the man was never one for physical labor. Peter walked into the dining room and heard Rhys in the kitchen, the soft sound of dishes being removed from water and placed in the rack to dry. He ran his fingers along the freshly polished table, wondering when Rhys bought the table runner. The flower vase looked nice, but rarely would Rhys would decorate the dining room table that way. He was always one for simplicity.

Peter pushed the kitchen door open, hearing the back door shut. The kitchen appeared spotless, but then again, Rhys always did keep it immaculate. The kitchen was the one room Peter stayed as far away from as possible. Rhys had a spot for every item, and nothing annoyed him faster than to have someone move his stuff. Something was wrong about the kitchen, though, something Peter couldn't quite put his finger on.

He walked across the kitchen and headed for the back door. "Rhys?"

Peter briefly caught sight of someone rounding the side of the house. The sun seemed so bright, brighter than normal. He raised his hand to shield his eyes as he walked along the porch, following Rhys. Peter turned around the corner of the house, the boards squeaking under his feet. He could see Rhys now, leaning over the railing, trying to reach something. He wondered briefly why he didn't just walk down the steps and pick up what he dropped.

"Rhys, sweetie, be careful, you're going to fall," he warned, but Rhys didn't act like he heard him.

"Rhys?" Peter called again. He turned as a strange man stepped around the corner. He was a large man, not so much in height but in build. If Peter had been writing about this he would have made the man a fighter, maybe a pro wrestler or something along that line. His shirt looked like it was straining to hold in all those muscles. The stranger's light-brown hair was in a buzz cut, almost military in nature.

"Who are you?" Peter demanded, walking toward the stranger.

The man didn't even acknowledge him. He stepped closer to Rhys, a large wooden paddle raised in the air. Rhys seemed unaware that the man was behind him.

"Rhys!" Peter called out a warning, rushing to stop the stranger from hitting Rhys. Almost as if everything happened in slow motion, he couldn't cover the space fast enough. He saw the paddle coming down and knew he wouldn't be able to get to Rhys before it slammed into his ass.

"Rhys!" he screamed as the paddle made contact with the upturned ass.

"Wake up, Peter."

"Rhys!" he screamed, flying up out of bed, momentarily disoriented.

"I'm here, sweetie." Rhys ran his hand down Peter's back, trying to comfort him.

The dream slowly receded to the back of Peter's mind, and the bedroom became clearer. He took a deep breath, his hands running over his face trying to fully wake up. He had never had a dream so violent before.

"You were dreaming, baby, thrashing about, calling out my name." He wrapped his arms around Peter's waist and rested his head on Peter's back.

"It was just a bad dream." Peter leaned back into the embrace. "I've just never had a dream so vivid, so real."

"Do you want to tell me about it?" Rhys whispered, his chin resting on Peter's shoulder.

Peter yawned. "I don't really remember what I was dreaming about. It's just flashes now—the dining room table with a gold-colored runner in the middle and a vase of yellow flowers."

Rhys kissed his shoulder, his teeth gently scraping over the flesh. "I can see why it's a nightmare. I'd never clutter my dining room table that way."

Peter lay back down, and Rhys laid his head on his chest. Rhys wiggled a little, trying to get comfortable and yet offer comfort at the same time.

"I should be able to remember my dream, but it's just out of my grasp, like I should have it, but I can't. All I get is the feeling of fear and helplessness."

Rhys slipped his fingers into Peter's short brown hair, his finger occasionally stroking the delicate earlobe. "It's probably not important. You're just a little overwhelmed by all the work that is going into the house, and it came out in the dream."

Peter closed his eyes and enjoyed the feel of the man he loved massaging his scalp. "It was nothing important, just a dream."

Rhys leaned forward and gently kissed his jaw before he snuggled back into Peter's shoulder. Peter sighed softly as he felt Rhys burrow into him, his arm instinctively pulling Rhys closer. It wasn't long before he drifted back to a deep, uneventful sleep.

"PETER, WAKE up, baby."

Peter began to stir, his arms automatically reaching for Rhys. He slid his hands along the satin sheets before pulling the pillow against his chest and snuggling a little deeper into the blankets.

"Come on, baby, this is getting heavy."

Peter rolled onto his back, where he stretched, spreading his legs wide and pointing his toes toward the wall. He raised his arms above his head, his back arching as his muscles protested the movement. Opening one eye, then the other, he reminded himself once more that they needed to buy curtains as the bright morning sun shone in through the window and directly onto the bed. He held his hand up, trying to block the blinding light, cursing the morning. He felt like he'd hardly slept a wink last night.

"Good morning, Peter."

"Morning," Peter mumbled sleepily, turning to see Rhys standing by the bed, holding a tray of food. "What is that?"

"I thought you might like breakfast in bed." Rhys watched as Peter scooted up until he sat with his back against the headboard. "You are aware that this is heavy."

Peter smoothed the blanket that pooled around his waist. He shifted a little, hoping Rhys noticed his morning wood. It might be nice to get a blow job after he had his breakfast—hell, while he ate breakfast would be good too.

"Good thing you covered that up. I worked too hard on breakfast for it to go cold." He set the tray in front of Peter as he kissed him.

"I think I'd rather have you for breakfast." Peter smiled devilishly as he moved the blanket aside to show just how hard he was.

"Nice try, but I'm still not impressed." Rhys held a piece of toast before Peter's mouth. "You eat and I'll head downstairs and finish cleaning up the kitchen."

"Well, I could move the tray over and you could suck me off while I eat breakfast." Peter waggled his eyebrows.

Rhys snorted. "I'm not sucking your cock. I think it can go a day or two without any oral stimulation from me."

"Stay with me, Rhys. Share this with me." Peter reached for him. "Just sit beside me."

"The kitchen needs cleaning. You know how I feel about anything being left a mess." He bit his lower lip as he sat on the bed beside Peter.

Peter took a bite of the toast, his hand sliding up and down the soft faded jeans that encased the slim legs until they could touch the smooth skin of Rhys's stomach. "Eat breakfast with me, Rhys. We'll clean the kitchen together."

Rhys tweaked his nose. "I know what you mean when you say *we* will clean it later—you mean *I'll* clean it later while you disappear."

Peter chuckled. Picking up a piece of bacon, he tested the crispiness of it before he took a bite.

"I burnt it just like you like it." Rhys rolled his eyes. He stood and walked toward the door. "I'll be in the kitchen if you need anything."

"Rhys?"

Rhys stopped in the doorway. "Yes, baby?"

Peter held up a piece of bacon. "Thank you, for everything."

Rhys gave him a big smile, the kind that wrinkled his nose and showed a set of beautiful straight white teeth. "You're more than welcome."

Peter propped the pillows behind him, leaned back against the headboard, and settled in for breakfast in bed. He really was lucky to have someone as great as Rhys. He smiled as he thought about the first time he saw the man who became his husband.

He had desperately needed some caffeine, so he'd walked into the coffee shop by the college. It had been a long hard day dealing with people at the bookstore, and a customer had pushed him to his last straight nerve. The little coffee shop was the closest to both work and college—one reason he hadn't entered it yet. After spending eight hours working with the public, the last thing he wanted was to hang out in a noisy coffee shop filled with college students. When he pushed open the door to the small coffee bar, the smell of freshly ground beans assaulted his senses and made his mouth water. He quickly found a seat in the corner.

The waiter had been the best thing about the place. His pale-blond hair cut in odd wedges reminded Peter of an anime character. The man had a tall lean body and eyes so blue he could lose himself in them. Peter had stared at the waiter the whole time, quickly trying to find something interesting about his coffee every time the man noticed him looking. He had wanted to ask the young man out, but he just didn't have the courage—asking someone out in person was a hell of a lot harder than in his books.

"Do you want to snap a picture of me? I mean, the way you were staring was almost like you were trying to commit me to memory," the waiter commented as Peter started to walk past him.

Peter had stood there like an idiot, his cheeks turning a bright red. He tried to talk, but all he managed was a pathetic squeak.

"You're pretty damn good-looking, even if you're a horrible conversationalist." He scrawled his number on a napkin and handed it to Peter. "My name is Rhys. Call me sometime and we can go out."

"Sure, yeah." Peter stumbled toward the door. Looking at the number written across the napkin, he was lucky he didn't run into anyone in his pathetic attempt to get out of the coffee shop before he made an idiot of himself. "I'll call tonight."

Rhys laughed. "I'll be waiting."

Peter grabbed the door as it was swinging shut. He could tell several people were staring at him, but at that moment he didn't really care. "I'm Peter."

Rhys laughed. "I'll be waiting by the phone, Peter, so you better call. I'd hate to be one of those pathetic guys who have to pick up the phone a dozen times to make sure it actually works."

Peter stepped back into the coffee shop when he realized he blocked the door. "What time do you get off?"

"Six."

Peter nodded. "I'll call by seven."

Calling Rhys had been the greatest thing he ever did. One date led to another, to late night phone calls, to sharing naughty pictures of each other—until he found he didn't want to spend life without Rhys. After five months, he asked Rhys to spend the rest of their lives together. He had been ecstatic when Rhys said yes, and eight years later, he was just as happy now as the day they committed to each other.

Peter finished eating his breakfast. He placed all of his dishes back on the tray, set it on the floor, and got out of bed. He shuddered as his feet hit the cold floor and reminded him he really needed to pee. Why could he lie in bed and not have the thought of peeing cross his mind, but the moment he sat up it was like all the pee ran to his bladder and demanded to come out now? He stood, and crossing his legs, he did a slight bouncing pee-pee dance before he crossed the room to the bathroom. Peter caught a glimpse of his reflection in the mirror over the sink as he made his way to the stool. His eyes had dark circles under them, his skin slightly pale. It really must be the stress of moving that gave him a sickly appearance.

As he peed, he looked at the dated wallpaper. Maybe he would tell Rhys the bathroom was the next room they needed to update. Peter was about ready to call in an interior designer. Forget doing all this work himself. It was more than one man could handle. Rhys had ideas, colors, pictures of flooring and so forth, but when it came to actually doing the work, he was more of an idea man. Peter was as handy as the next guy, but they could afford an interior decorator—someone who would show them swatches of colors, who would take Rhys's ideas of simplicity and his ideas of modern art and somehow combine them. The more he thought about the idea, the more he liked it. Peter always wanted to be the man who picked out furniture and other bits of décor and had them all magically appear in his house exactly where they all looked perfect.

He finger combed his short, spiky brown hair. He needed to shave, but since he didn't plan on leaving the house, he would wait to do that. He walked back into the bedroom, grabbed a pair of jeans and a T-shirt from the dresser, and pulled them on. Then he picked up the tray with his dirty dishes—he would take them down to Rhys. He smiled. It would probably give Rhys a heart attack that he brought the dishes down and didn't leave them up there for Rhys to get later.

Peter began to whistle as he walked down the stairs—okay, maybe whistling was a strong word. He wanted to, he really did, but the song that came past his lips was a lot more monotone than the one in his head. He wasn't sure who was worse at whistling, him or Rhys. They both loved to whistle. Hell, if the mood was right, they would both sing rather off-key but with much enthusiasm as they danced around the house.

He crossed the highly polished wooden floor and had to admit the wood did look nice. Glad they had spent so much time cleaning it, not that he would admit that to Rhys, he pushed open the door to the kitchen, carefully easing the tray past the doorframe. The last thing he wanted was to carry it this far only to hit the doorjamb and drop it all over the floor.

"Thank you for bringing it down." Rhys walked over to take the tray from him, giving him a quick kiss in the process. "I figured I'd have to go up and get it."

Peter grinned. "I know you did, but I thought I'd surprise you and actually do something without you telling me to."

Rhys laughed as he started to rinse off the dishes in the sink. For some odd reason, Rhys always washed the dishes before he placed them in the dishwasher. "Well, thank you for thinking about me. It's about time you carried a dish into the kitchen. Is this going to be the start of a new trend?"

"You know, I was thinking we should hire an interior designer to finish the house for us." Peter refilled his cup of coffee, completely ignoring Rhys's last remark.

"No, Peter, I want this to be all us." Rhys glanced at him as he placed the dishes in the dishwasher.

"The bathrooms need to be updated. I know nothing about plumbing." He took a sip of the rich, dark liquid.

Rhys turned from the sink. He grabbed a towel from where it hung and dried off his hands. "Of course we can call in a plumber, but the actual painting and design I want to be us. We'll put all the furniture in the front room in place, and you will be amazed at how good it looks. You'll be able to stand back and say we did this."

Peter gave a soft sigh of defeat. "So we're going to give the wood one more quick polish, move the furniture where we want it, paint the dining room, and finish the kitchen?"

Rhys sashayed over to Peter. Placing his arms around Peter's neck, he rubbed their noses together. "I think we can skip polishing the wood. I tell you what, you help me move the furniture around the front room, and I'll do the rest of the stuff."

"The rest of the stuff?"

Rhys nodded. "You can go write, rest outside, or something, and I'll paint the dining room. You don't look good, Peter. Your skin is pale, and your eyes look like I've beaten you."

"Everyone knows how mean you can be to me," Peter teased, nuzzling Rhys's jawline before he placed a quick kiss on it.

Rhys slapped Peter's arm as he pulled out of Peter's grasp. "If I beat you, it's because you need it."

"Can we tell people that we had wild kinky sex that got a little out of hand?"

Rhys laughed. "Sure. People would really believe that. Hell, the other night when we were with Sam and Mike, the subject of S and M came up, and I thought you were going to turn three shades of green. Hey, maybe that could be the name of your next bestseller, *Fifty Shades of Green: One Man's Voyage into Kinky Sex*."

"My editor said I needed to branch out to a little light S and M. The market is growing in that area. Maybe we were experimenting, so I could write about it in my book."

Rhys shook his head as he began to put the dry dishes away. He never placed pans in the dishwasher, something else Peter could never figure out. He knew they had a small economy-size one, but to Peter it washed pots and pans as well as everything else.

"No one would believe the story, baby." Rhys smiled as he placed a pan under the counter.

"Fine, I still think it would be fun to tell people that, though. You know what, I'll help paint the dining room. It'll go faster if we both do it." Peter walked over to Rhys and snuggled into his arms. "The kitchen is all you, though. No way in hell I'll be in here while you organize."

Rhys laughed as he wrapped his arms around Peter. "What are you hinting at?"

"Nothing." Peter stepped away, trying to look innocent. "I'd never accuse you of being a bit anal when it comes to the kitchen."

"I like people to clean up the mess they make and put things back where they got them. I don't believe that is being anal."

Peter kissed his cheek, patting Rhys's ass as he stepped around him. "I'll go get the paint and the brushes."

"I'll be there in just a couple of minutes." He opened one of the boxes that sat on the floor. "I'm going to put a roast in the Crock-Pot so it will be done for supper."

"Sounds good."

Chapter 4

"I DIDN'T know painting could be such a tiring job." Peter pulled his paint-covered shirt off and tossed it toward the wastebasket. "No use keeping that shirt. It's ruined."

"I didn't know you could get so much paint on yourself. Did you manage to get any of it on the walls?" Rhys teased, lifting Peter's arm. "Tell me, how did you get paint under your arm like that?"

Peter raised his arm to see what Rhys was talking about. He managed to see a streak of gray very close to his armpit. "Look who's talking. You have it on your forehead, your nose, and who knows where else. Maybe I better remove your clothes and inspect you myself."

"Yeah, I probably do have it on my face, but that's just because I kept pushing my hair out of my eyes. I really need to get it cut."

"Don't you dare. I love the geometric angles." He ran his fingers through Rhys's too-long bangs. "Your hair is freaking artistic."

"Artistic?" Rhys raised one eyebrow.

"Yeah, artists always have the coolest hair, and you're an artist and gamer, so it means you have to have an extracool haircut." Peter placed a quick kiss on Rhys's soft, full lips.

Rhys laughed. "So, if I was a construction worker, then I'd need to have a buzz cut?"

"If you get a buzz cut, I'm so leaving you." Peter stepped away from Rhys. He gave an exaggerated full-body shudder as if the thought of a buzz cut was a fate worse than death.

"I'm glad you love me so unconditionally," Rhys teased.

"Hey, I said for better or worse, rich or poor. I never mentioned bad haircuts," Peter pointed out. He really tried to look serious, but failed.

"You know, your hair isn't that far off a buzz cut," Rhys pointed out. "You don't see me shuddering every time you come back from getting your hair done."

"You know, if we were into kinky sex, now is the time I would beat your ass red." Peter crossed his arms over his chest and cocked one eyebrow as he looked at Rhys.

Rhys turned, shaking his ass in front of Peter. "Go ahead, show me. I've been a bad boy."

Peter rolled his eyes. "For your information, my haircut is one of the more popular ones today. I may not be as artsy as you, but I still stay stylish."

Rhys crossed the short distance to him and smiled as he kissed Peter's forehead. "Yes, sweetie, you're always stylish and professional. I love you for that. Do you want to get your office set up before we go to bed?"

Peter shook his head. "I've got my desk set up and the computer in there. Anything else can wait."

"Are you sure?" He slid his arms around Peter's waist. "We're on a roll here. We might as well get as much done as possible."

"I think we need to quit while we're ahead. Moving your desk to the attic was a bitch. We really should have called some friends in to help with that."

"Hey, I can carry heavy crap as well as the next guy," Rhys protested, his bottom lip thrusting out as he pouted.

"Which is why when we moved the bed frame you complained the whole time just how heavy it was and you were getting calluses?"

Rhys ran his hands up Peter's bare back. "Well, when I give you those late-night hand jobs, you don't want me to scratch up your penis by having really rough sandpaper hands, do you?"

Peter kissed the tip of his nose. "Of course not. You know one of the things I like about you is those very long artistic fingers."

"These hands were made for loving, not for hard work," Rhys agreed.

"Am I going to get to break the bedroom in tonight?" Peter asked. "You can remind me that those loving hands shouldn't be forced to work by letting the more tender parts of my body experience their smooth silkiness."

Rhys shrugged, pulling away from Peter he walked toward the bathroom. "The first thing I'm going to do is wash some of this paint and grime from my skin."

"If you would let me hire someone to finish the remodeling, we could have a nice big shower installed."

Rhys sashayed across the bedroom, looking over his shoulder and smiling wickedly. "We could do that, or we could take advantage of the fact that the older tubs are much bigger than the newer ones."

"So I might get lucky after all?" Peter waggled his eyebrows.

Rhys peered back around the doorjamb. "Not if you don't get in here."

Peter almost broke the sound barrier as he ran to the bathroom and skidded to a halt beside the tub.

"I'm surprised you didn't shed your jeans on the run in here." Rhys sat on the edge of the marble tub testing the water with his wrist as he filled it. "Should I add bubbles?"

"Nah, no bubbles." Peter placed his hand behind Rhys's neck and leaned down to kiss him. He ran his tongue across Rhys's soft, full lips before pushing into his hot mouth.

Rhys moaned. Tilting his head back to deepen the kiss knocked him off-balance and caused him to fall into the tub. The look of shock on his face brought a fit of laughter from Peter. He held out his hand and helped Rhys out of the tub.

"Glad you found that funny." Rhys stood, dripping on the floor.

"Let's face it, if it had been me, you would have laughed too."

Rhys shed the dripping clothes.

"Come on, sexy baby." Peter stripped off his jeans. "Let's get in the tub and relax."

"Just a second." He scooped up the wet items and deposited them into the sink.

Peter eased into the hot water and settled against the back of the tub. He held out his hand.

"I should have put bubbles in," Rhys commented, standing by the edge of the tub.

"You haven't turned off the water yet. If you really want some, add them."

Rhys grabbed the bubble bath off the shelf and dumped a rather generous amount into the water. Using his hand, he vigorously moved the water back and forth, bringing white bubbles to the surface. When he was satisfied with what he saw, he allowed Peter to help him into the hot water.

"I'm not sure what feels better at the moment, the hot water relaxing my muscles or your body nestled in my arms," Peter whispered in Rhys's ear. He placed a small kiss on Rhys's delicate lobe.

Rhys leaned back so his head lay against Peter's shoulder. Closing his eyes, he reached down and entwined his fingers with Peter's. "The water feels so good. I swear I can feel the dirt and dust just lifting from my body. At this moment in my life, I feel so safe and relaxed."

Peter kissed his temple. "I promise to always keep you safe, to always protect you for as long as I can take a breath."

A smile spread across Rhys's face. "Thank you for buying me the house, baby. I know it isn't your first choice, but we can really make this place a home. I can see us living the rest of our lives here, little ninety-year-old men in rockers on the front porch watching the sunset."

Peter squeezed his fingers, moving his thumb in small circles around Rhys's belly button. "I'll still think you're the sexiest man alive and want sex on a weekly basis."

"Weekly?" Rhys chuckled. "Do you think you'll still be able to get it up so often?"

"If I have to strap a stick to it, I'll be hard and ready for you," Peter solemnly vowed.

"Ah Peter, why can I picture that?"

"Because you know it's true." He placed a battery of kisses on Rhys's exposed shoulder.

Rhys reached over, grabbed the washcloth and body wash, and handed them to Peter. "Please wash my back, baby."

"I don't want you to leave my arms," Peter protested.

"The sooner you wash my back, the sooner I'll be snuggled into your arms." Rhys slid forward to give better access.

Peter squirted some body wash onto the cloth. Working a small lather into the material, he started to wash Rhys's back. He used small strokes, starting at one shoulder then moving down along the spine and back up again. After a few moments he dropped the washcloth in the water. He watched as the warm water cascaded over Rhys's back, washing away the soap. He began to rub Rhys's back, his fingers massaging the kinks from the tight muscles. Rhys gave a low moan and scooted forward a little, hugging his knees to give Peter better access. Peter ran his hands up and down the long lean back, his fingers kneading the tense muscles.

"I have aches where I didn't know I could ache." Rhys flinched as Peter hit a sore spot.

"Manual labor just isn't your thing. You're lucky that you're so damn sexy."

"Sexy has nothing to do with it. I thought you were sexy as hell when I saw you in the coffee shop. I said, there's a man who will not only take care of me, but looks like he'll do all the manual labor around the house."

Peter laughed. "You got all that out of the first sighting?"

"Rub my shoulders a little more, baby."

Peter moved his hands up, his fingers kneading the tense muscles. He could feel Rhys relaxing under his hands. "You lean forward a little more, and I can think of someplace else I'll massage."

"I think I'll pass."

Peter shook his head. "If you wish. Lean back, baby, and I'll rub your chest."

Rhys slid back until he pressed against Peter's chest. Peter slid his arms down until he held Rhys while the hot water relaxed both their muscles. Sometimes it was nice to just hold Rhys. Peter could forget about everything—the stress of his day, the problems in writing. Everything just disappeared.

"You know, I don't think I have ever heard silence like this. When we lived in the duplex, we could hear Mrs. White every time she was in the bathroom," Rhys commented.

"It's a bit eerie, really. How many horror stories have we watched that happen in a house just like this? The woman is always in the bathtub enjoying the hot water and silence when something happens. The ghost will either yank her under, blood will start dripping from the faucet, or doors will slam."

Rhys laughed. "You watch way too much TV, you know that."

"I know I do." Peter sighed deeply. "I got an e-mail from my editor."

"What did Vickie want?"

"Not a lot. She mentioned that while my books have steady sales, she thinks maybe I need to start adding a little bondage to my stories. She says kink is hot, and I should branch out that way."

"What did you say?"

"That I know nothing about being kinky." Peter moved his hands from Rhys's stomach to his cock.

"Yeah, I can attest to that."

"You're not saying no?" Peter ran the washcloth over the delicate orbs, noticing Rhys's cock twitch.

"I didn't say you were getting sex. I'm just not stopping a little petting."

Peter kissed his cheek, slowly sliding his hand up and down Rhys's cock. It responded to the slow strokes, the roughness of the terry material.

"Damn, baby, keep that up, and I'll fall asleep," Rhys murmured.

"I still think you should get on your hands and knees and let me fuck you."

"In the water?"

"Yeah, baby, let's make waves."

Rhys chuckled softly. "I hope you don't use that line in one of your books."

He pretended to look hurt, not that Rhys could see it. "I think that was one of my best lines, and believe me, if I use it in my book the character would be more than willing to put out."

"I think we should get out of the tub and get in bed before I fall asleep against you." Rhys opened his eyes and sat up. He reached for the washcloth and ran it quickly over his legs.

"Would that be all that bad?" Peter asked, skimming his finger down his lover's back.

"No, it wouldn't be." Rhys rose from the tub, Peter's hand sliding along his hip as he did. "But I don't want to fall asleep in the tub."

"Come on, baby. Let's stay in the warm water a little while longer."

Rhys paused at the edge. "If I stay in the tub, I'll fall asleep. If I fall asleep, there is no way you're getting lucky tonight."

"I don't care about getting lucky tonight, I just want to hold you."

Rhys smiled softly. "Hold me tonight in bed. Let me rest against you, feel the mattress easing the aches from my body while I'm safe in your arms."

"Are you sure you're not the writer? That was one of the most romantic lines I've heard in a while. Remind me to put that in a book, all right?"

"All gamers are storytellers." He ran the towel over his body. "I do have to admit that line was better than 'let's make waves.'"

"I still think you should grab the edge of the tub and let me fuck you senseless."

Rhys wrapped the towel around his waist. "That's not happening."

"You can't fault me for trying." Peter stood. He took a moment to run the towel up and down his legs, knowing Rhys would stop what he was doing and watch him move.

"You have a great body," Rhys whispered, reaching out to touch Peter.

"I'm glad you like what you see." Straightening, Peter fastened the towel around his waist. "Go get in bed, and I'll be in there as soon as I shave."

"You don't have to shave." Rhys ran his fingers across Peter's jawline, feeling the stubble of the day's growth.

"Are you sure?"

Rhys nodded, and placing his hand on the side of Peter's face, he leaned in to give him a soft kiss. Peter moaned against Rhys's lips, his hand slipping into the wet hair and pulling the man closer, his lips parting as they came together.

"I'm getting into bed." Rhys turned and hurried across the wooden floors to the bed.

Peter leaned against the bathroom doorframe. "I think you are so sexy when you snuggle under the blanket like that. It's the whole reason I don't mind when you stick your cold feet on me."

"Well, the wood floor is cold. The sheets are cold. Hell, I'm wet and cold. We need to buy an electric blanket or something."

"Maybe I can figure out a way to warm you up," Peter offered.

Rhys fluffed the blanket a little. "If you weren't trying to get laid daily, I'd think something was wrong."

Peter crawled onto the bed, the towel he had wrapped around his waist falling open. He grabbed the blanket and pulled it from Rhys's body. The man still had the towel wrapped around his waist. "I never can get the thing to stay around my waist. I don't see how you do."

"Surprised you wore that in here anyway." Rhys lay on the bed, and using his toe, he pushed the towel the rest of the way open.

Grabbing Rhys's foot with one hand, Peter used his free hand to toss the towel on the floor.

Rhys ran his free foot along Peter's thigh, a seductive smile on his face as he skimmed his nails over his own chest. Peter took hold of the foot and massaged Rhys's arch. Rhys wiggled a little on the bed, getting comfortable, his eyes closed as he felt his whole body relax. He continued to stroke his chest, pinching his nipples, bringing them to full hard points.

"You have great feet," Peter whispered, leaning forward to put the big toe in his mouth. He swirled his tongue around the toe as he sucked. He really did have a bit of a foot fetish, one that Rhys was more than willing to let him indulge.

Peter sucked on the toe, enjoying the contrasting textures—the smooth hardness of the nail, the rough skin on the bottom of the toe, the softness between them. Exhaling softly, he began to suck on it as he would a cock.

"Damn that's good." Rhys moaned, one hand pinching his nipple and the other running in small circles around his belly button.

Peter moved off the toe and ran his fingers all over the foot, pressing against the pressure point and watching, as Rhys seemed to melt under the massage.

"You have the most magical fingers." Rhys moaned. "Make sure you pay as much attention to the rest of my body as you do my feet."

"Change feet." Peter let go of one and reached for the other. He began to use his thumbs to massage the second foot before leaning down to suck on a toe. He moved from one toe to the other, gently sucking each one, occasionally taking two in his mouth.

"You know I have ticklish feet." Rhys giggled as Peter ran his tongue along the arch.

Peter moved back up and took the large toe in his mouth. He continued to suck, running his fingers along the smooth, freshly shaved leg.

"I shaved them just for you." Rhys smiled wickedly. "It's not the only place I shaved either."

"Really? What did I miss? Hell, how did I miss the shaved legs?" Peter cocked one eyebrow.

Rhys giggled. "You missed it because I washed my own legs and you were trying too hard to get me to bend over the tub to notice that I shaved my underarms also."

"Well, I guess I'll have to explore your body with my tongue to see what else I might have missed."

"You might have to do that."

Peter began to kiss Rhys's slim ankles, his tongue sliding over the anklebone before he returned to small little kisses. He ran his nails over his bare leg, and Rhys shuddered in pleasure. He kissed and nipped his way up to the knee. Peter began to run his nails under the back of his leg, watching as Rhys jerked when Peter hit a ticklish spot.

"You have a lot of ticklish spots."

"And after eight years you have found them all," Rhys acknowledged.

"Do you think I should explore your body again to make sure I didn't miss one? After all, I didn't notice that you had shaved your legs or under your arms."

"Only if it involves your tongue."

Peter settled between Rhys's spread legs admiring the view for a few moments. He grabbed hold of Rhys's legs, hooked his arms under his knees, and scooted Rhys down until the man's ass was pressed firmly against his crotch. He reached up to rub Rhys's chest and ran the flats of his palms along Rhys's stomach—watching Rhys's muscles twitch as he laughed—and up and over his nipples, feeling the hard nubs under his hands. He skimmed his fingers along Rhys's side, causing the man to twitch as he hit a ticklish spot. Peter continued his strokes, up along Rhys's chest, rubbing his nipples, and back down along Rhys's side while his hips gently rocked forward, pushing his hard cock against Rhys's bare ass, letting it slip between Rhys's asscheeks and skim over his hole but never entering him.

Peter leaned forward, pushing Rhys's legs up to his chest. He leaned down to kiss Rhys and forced his tongue past his lips and into the hot sweet mouth. Peter continued to grind against Rhys, his cock finding a steady rhythm in the crack of Rhys's full, round ass, as Rhys began to rock, matching Peter's thrusting.

"Fuck me!" Rhys cried out. "Put your dick up my ass!"

"I'm not sure we are ready for that yet." Peter stopped his thrusting, and pulling back a little, he calmed his breathing.

"We're more than ready for that." Rhys grabbed at him, wanting to pull him close.

"Not yet, sweetie."

"Please, baby, fuck me." Rhys reached over and grabbed the lube from the nightstand and tossed it toward Peter.

"I still think I should play with you a while longer," Peter teased as he opened the bottle and squeezed some lube on his cock.

"I think if you ever want sex again, you better get that damn thing in me." He tossed his legs over Peter's shoulders.

Peter smiled. He reached between Rhys's legs and inserted his finger in the tight hole, working it in and out. He eased the second finger in, watching as Rhys tensed for the briefest moment before relaxing into the fingers. After a few moments, he lined his cock up with Rhys and pushed his way in. Rhys groaned loudly in pleasure.

"Damn, baby, every time I enter you it's like the first time." Peter began to gently rock against Rhys.

"Less talking, more fucking," Rhys growled, bucking his hips up against Peter.

Peter began thrusting harder and faster. He put a roll to his hips, making sure he not only hit that special spot in Rhys, but all the special spots he had. Peter winced a little as Rhys dug his nails into his arms, but he soon forgot the pain as he started to lose himself in the sensation. He leaned down and thrust his tongue into Rhys's mouth, feeling the man lock his ankles around his waist. Rhys fisted Peter's hair and pulled a little as he pressed his lips hard against Peter's. They would have bruises from the force of the kiss later, but Peter didn't give a damn. Rhys raked his nails down Peter's back.

"Oh fuck, do that again!" Peter screamed out.

"I'm close!" Rhys cried out.

Peter pounded harder, the whole bed moving with the force of his thrusts. "Oh God! I'm almost there, baby."

"Oh God!" Rhys bit into Peter's shoulder as his orgasm ripped through his body.

"Fuck!" Peter screamed out, the pain from the bite enough to send him over the edge of ecstasy.

"Oh my God, baby, that was fucking good," Rhys panted.

Peter rolled off him to lie on his back. Rhys turned onto his side to snuggle close to him. Peter wrapped his arm around Rhys, who curled against him, Rhys's nose just under his jawline. It wasn't long before he felt Rhys's steady breathing fluttering against his neck.

Peter ran his hand over Rhys's hip. He could feel the heaviness in his limbs, but his mind didn't seem to want to slow down enough to sleep. Outside, an owl hooted and a dog howled, but sleep just wasn't coming to him. He glanced at the moon shining bright in the window. He loved full moon nights. When he looked out the window, he always got the greatest story ideas. He used to wonder what it was like to live somewhere where he could stare at the night sky without the interference of the bright city lights. He chuckled. Well, thanks to Rhys he now had the answer to that question. Other than the light on the pole to mark their driveway, no other lights shone outside. He could turn in a full circle and never see his neighbor's house.

He glanced at the clock and noticed it was 11:00 p.m. Peter closed his eyes, willing sleep to come. The moment he closed his eyes, all his stories invaded his brain. He could picture the sirens sitting on the rocks, luring the sailors toward them. He could see a red-haired man running in blinding white snow, a wagon train full of gay men traveling across the plains.

"Sleep, Peter, you need to sleep," he muttered. He shifted a little, causing Rhys to murmur something and snuggle closer. Peter kissed the top of his head. Still, sleep eluded him. He thought about all the open calls his publisher had coming up. Maybe he should start plotting out some of those stories. He shook his head. What the hell was he doing? He already had three series; the last thing he needed was to add more. He couldn't help it, though—his mind was too chaotic, his imagination in constant overdrive, and sometimes the simplest things made him think of whole new story ideas. He opened his eyes and looked at the clock only to notice half an hour had passed. Peter sighed; he might as well get some work done. He gently pulled his arm from under Rhys, trying not to wake him.

"What's wrong, baby?" Rhys mumbled sleepily.

"I can't sleep." Peter threw back the covers. "I'm going to write for a little bit."

"Sex will make you tired." Rhys let his fingers run down Peter's side.

"Go back to sleep, honey. We had enough sex less than an hour ago." Peter grabbed Rhys's hand. Bringing it to his lips, he kissed Rhys's fingers. "I'll be back in bed before you know it. I have a few deadlines approaching, and that is probably the reason for my restlessness."

"Are you sure?" Rhys asked, pulling the blankets up a little higher. "I might be willing to do it again, if it's as good as it was earlier."

Peter chuckled. "More than sure, darling."

"Okay," he mumbled sleepily.

Peter stared at Rhys a moment longer. Rhys was as handsome today as he had been eight years ago. He touched Rhys's soft, silky hair. He was the luckiest man alive and he knew it. How many men would put up with Peter's odd little quirks and love him unconditionally? Peter knew they had a love that came along once in a lifetime—the kind of love many people looked for but never found. After tucking the blankets around Rhys a little tighter, he tiptoed over to the dresser to grab a pair of sweats.

He pulled the bedroom door mostly closed behind him, leaving it open just a crack. It really was dark in the hallway. They needed to invest in several nightlights. He had been raised in the city, and even when all the lights were off, the lights of the city still filtered into the house. Out here, only the moon and stars shone. The ghost stories that he often watched suddenly entered his thought, every creaking board becoming the footsteps of a serial killer.

His body gave an involuntary shudder. He was spooking himself, and he knew it. He reached into the spare room and flipped the switch, filling the room with light. He glanced around the bare room. Maybe tomorrow he would get around to finishing the office. His desk was really the only thing he had set up—his computer in the middle and a ton of paper scattered across it. No matter how hard he tried to keep his desk clean, it was always cluttered.

Peter walked across the room, his footsteps echoing as he crossed to the window. After pushing aside the curtain, he looked at the night sky. The stars were so bright out here, and the moon seemed larger and rounder than when they lived in the city. The moon shone through the trees now. He tilted his head to one side and thought about the moon. He could use it in several stories—a witch flying across the face, a wolf howling under it, or a prisoner looking at it through the bars of a dungeon. He stared at it a moment longer, an idea forming. Happy that his writer's block seemed to be passing, he turned quickly and walked to his computer.

He pulled out his chair. He cleared off his desk, sweeping the half-eaten bag of chips into the trash.

"Why can you never stay clean?" he muttered to himself as he continued to drop pop cans and candy wrappers into the basket. He had a bad habit of snacking when he wrote. A can of pop soon became two or three, and a handful of chips became half a bag as he continued to snack and type. After he cleaned off his desk, he sat down to write.

"What to work on tonight?" he whispered, his voice rather loud in the fairly empty room. He opened his file folder of stories in progress. Surely one of them would be willing to talk to him tonight. If not, he did have the new idea in his head. Peter closed his eyes for a moment. He pictured a dark-haired boy, thin and waifish. The young man stared out the window, looking at the moon and wondering if someone out there was thinking about him, dreaming of loving him.

"Would you love me? Would you protect me?"

Peter could almost hear the whispered voice. It even held an accent, something that Peter loved.

"Yes," he whispered. "I'd keep you safe. I'd love you."

The man standing beside the window turned to look at him. "You would have loved me?"

"Yes, I would have loved you," Peter responded, studying the full lips and the brown eyes that seemed too big for his heart-shaped face.

The man focused on something over Peter's shoulder, his eyes growing wide with fear. Then he ran, and a cold breeze blew through the room, ruffling Peter's hair and knocking over his trash can.

Peter opened his eyes with a start. It was a great scene for a book. Now if he could just get it from his mind to the computer before any of it faded. He noticed the trash can lying on its side. Reaching down to pick it up, he briefly wondered when he'd knocked it over.

Somewhere downstairs, he heard a thump, like someone had fallen. Peter glanced over his shoulder as the hair on his arms stood on end. He breathed deeply, calming his nerves. The stairs creaked—it sounded almost like someone was walking up the wooden steps. The footfall was heavy; it reminded him of a man wearing hard-soled shoes or maybe even boots.

"Rhys?" he called over his shoulder. He waited a moment, expecting Rhys to answer, to step around the corner.

Peter sat for a moment, listening for any signs of Rhys moving about. He shook his head. He was letting his imagination get the best of him. Houses made noise—that was a fact. The sound of someone walking up the steps was nothing more than the house settling.

Peter stared at his computer. Ten minutes ago he couldn't stop his overactive mind from giving him scenes for a story, and now nothing more than a sentence or two would come. Usually he had no problem coming up with stories. His editor knew he would produce at least four books a year. He was her go-to guy whenever they didn't get the books they needed for an open call. He always had something in the works, some harebrained idea, most of which were so odd they never became a story. His mind was a scary place. Rhys teased him, saying he could mention a rubber duck and it would make Peter think of haunted houses. One of the reasons he had such a strong fan base was that he never wrote what most mainstream authors did. He tended to walk to the beat of his own drummer. He had once thought he should write the mainstream stuff, but Rhys had encouraged his individuality.

Rolling his shoulders, he let out a frustrated sigh. "You can do this, Peter. Just pick a story and start typing. You can always delete what you don't like later."

"Peter?"

Peter jumped at the sound of his name, more a whispered sigh than spoken. He pushed his chair back a little and turned to see if

45

Rhys had gotten out of bed. Perhaps Rhys was talking in his sleep. He often did that.

"Rhys, honey?" Peter called. Silence answered him again. He rose from his chair and walked across the bare floor, wishing he had worn socks. He peeked out into the hallway, checking for Rhys. The hallway stood just as dark and empty as when he'd first walked down it. "Are you okay, honey?"

He stared down the hallway, holding his breath as he strained to hear even the slightest sound. Perhaps he had only heard Rhys roll over, a rustle of blankets but nothing more. He tilted his head to one side. The shadows seemed different than they had before, darker, with a more solid shape. He stepped into the hallway to get a better look. His heart beat loudly, and his skin tingled as goose bumps started to rise on his forearms. The shadow seemed to loom at the end of the corridor—if a shadow could loom.

"It's a full moon," he told himself. "The moonlight shining through the window caused shadows."

A chill passed over his body. He shuddered, rubbing his arms for warmth as he walked back into his office. Almost as soon as he felt the cool air, it vanished. Peter sighed deeply, shaking his head as he did. He wrote paranormal romance. He couldn't let his imagination get the better of him. He walked back to his computer.

"You just moved in, Peter, you're letting a beautiful house spook you. It's just like when you moved into the duplex. New places always creep you out until you get used to them."

Shaking his head slightly, he turned back to his computer, and taking a deep breath to calm his nerves, he began to type.

"Run!"

They jumped up, scattering among the rocks. Meelo grabbed her daughter's hand and ran for the water. She glanced at her husband, who grabbed Kyto and held the toddler against his chest as he also ran for the water, glancing at his people, looking for his other sons.

"Make for the water!" he called to his people. They would find safety in the caves below the surface. No mortal could swim so far down.

"Help!"

Lyall stopped.

"Go, Dad. I'll help him." Destin waved his father on as he ran back for his brother.

The sailor held Dax around the waist, trying to pull a dirty burlap bag over his head.

"Help me, Destin!" Dax screamed, twisting and kicking the man who held him.

A shrill scream filled the room, yanking Peter out of his story. He flew up from his chair, knocking it over in the process. A chill skittered down his spine, and goose bumps rose. He looked out the doorway. The hallway seemed darker than it had earlier. Before, he had been able to make out the shape of the vase and table, but now there was a solid inky blackness, as if someone blocked the light. He needed to check on Rhys, make sure he wasn't calling out because he had a bad dream.

Peter stared at the doorway, trying to force himself to take a step forward. All the while, every fiber in his body told him to close the door, turn on the radio, and make some kind of noise so whatever was in the hall would flee. He chuckled a little, like the sound of a radio would cause an intruder to flee. He stepped forward, his body giving an involuntary shudder.

"If there's something in the hall, I need to go out there and protect Rhys," he told himself, his voice sounding unusually loud.

He sighed once more. Firmly nodding, he steeled his nerves and stepped out of the office. Nothing was there. The moon lit up the hallway that had seemed so dark from the office. Shadows moved as clouds passed over the moon, but other than that, he saw clearly. He walked down the hallway to their bedroom. When he reached out to push open the door, he was surprised how badly his hand was shaking. It wasn't like anything was in the house. Rhys was sleeping, probably having a bad dream. Rhys lay asleep, the moonlight shining through the window to illuminate his face. Peter leaned against the doorframe, watching his lover. Rhys looked so beautiful—the way the moon reflected off his skin, his blond hair tousled in sleep, and his soft full lips slightly parted, still a bit puffy from their lovemaking. Rhys licked his lips, giving a soft sigh as he rolled over, his arm reaching across the bed to find Peter. Rhys frowned slightly in his sleep, his arm going out a little farther.

Peter smiled, walked across the room, and reached out to stroke Rhys's hair, to push a lock that had fallen into his face behind his ear. Rhys sighed as he settled back into deep sleep, content that Peter was there.

"I love you, baby," Peter whispered, placing a kiss on Rhys's cheek.

Making sure Rhys was tucked in, Peter walked back to his office. The sounds had been the house settling. The sound of his name was nothing more than a branch brushing against the outside walls. He needed to get used to the sounds of the country and stop spooking himself. He was going to hear things out here that he didn't hear in the city.

Peter sat in front of his computer and pulled up each of his stories. He would write something tonight. He grabbed his MP3 player and plugged it into the computer. The music would drown out the calls of animals, the creaks of the house, and anything else that would distract him.

Chapter 5

"COFFEE?" RHYS held up a cup.

Peter shook his head, stumbling toward the kitchen table. He wasn't a morning person—never had been. He fell heavily into the chair, mumbling a good morning as Rhys moved to the refrigerator to get him a glass of juice.

"Did you get a lot written last night?" Rhys asked as he placed the glass in front of Peter. "I swear you got up three times."

"I couldn't sleep. I kept dreaming something, but I couldn't remember it the moment I woke up. I figured I might as well do a little writing, but even then I couldn't concentrate." He took a sip of the cold liquid and winced as it went down. "I'm lucky if I got a thousand words written."

"Do you want me to fix you anything for breakfast?"

Peter shook his head. "I can fix some toast later if I want it. You know the oddest thing about sitting in the new office and writing? I kept feeling like someone was watching me. You don't know how many times I turned around to look to see if you were there."

"Don't you say you can usually see the people you're writing about, almost like they are sitting beside you?"

"No, not like this. When I write, I see them walk up to me. They stand leaning against the doorframe or sit on the edge of the desk." He pursed his lips in thought. He was glad Rhys understood what he meant. Other people might want him committed for comments like that. "This was different. There was something tangible about this feeling."

"It's still a new house, baby. You aren't used to having such a large room to work in. Are you going to paint the walls with the washable paint?" Rhys wiped the counter down with a damp cloth.

Peter nodded, taking another drink of his juice. This time it went down easier. "I keep track of the stories, ideas, and people better if I can look at the wall and see the character flow."

"Once you get the office fully set up the way you want it, the room won't feel so empty. Believe me, I was in the attic the other afternoon painting, and the whole thing echoed. I felt like I was being watched, too, but it was just because the place was empty. I'll get my drawings up there—my posters, life size cutouts of my game characters—and the office will feel like home and not an empty room."

"Yeah, you're right." Peter sighed. "How's your office coming along?"

Rhys slid the chair out and sat down. "I really like the color I chose. I was afraid the purple would be too bright, but you know, with that cream you picked out, it just seems perfect. I've got my posters up, and I plan on getting the character sketches for the newest game up today."

"Sounds like you'll be busy."

Rhys smiled. "I know we still have the rest of the house to finish up, but I figured that once our offices are done, then we can get back to work. We need a break from painting and peeling wallpaper and buffing floors."

"The appeal of interior design wearing off already?" Peter teased.

Rhys gave a one-shoulder shrug. "You know me, everything is great the first two days."

"Then your little chaotic mind wanders off to new projects. I know now why you married someone so good with his hands." Peter reached across the table to touch Rhys's hand. He traced his finger in small circles on the back.

"That's not the only reason I chose someone who knew how to use his hands." Rhys smiled wickedly.

"Yes, you reminded me many times last night how good I was with my hands. I think I like the fact that we have no neighbors. You can scream out your passion for me much louder and longer now."

Rhys finished off his coffee. "I have yet to be too hoarse to talk the next day. You've promised to make me that way for eight years. Now that we live in the country I expect you to make good on your promise."

Peter chuckled. "That sounds like a challenge, and you know how much I like a challenge."

Rhys smiled. He pushed away from the table, turned, and put his coffee mug in the sink. "It's going to be a beautiful day. I think I might spend some of it outside, maybe clean off the porch. I'm going to open all the windows downstairs and really air out the house."

Peter looked at the bright-blue sky through the window. "I think I'll write outside today. I didn't get to do that much back in the city, but here the beautiful day calls to you."

"I have the yard furniture set up in that little cluster of trees. I figured it would give us shade when the sun was overhead, and, well, I thought the area was beautiful."

Peter laughed. He slid back his chair, grabbed his glass off the table, and carried it to the sink. "I don't care where the yard furniture is set. Hell, I'd be just as happy to sit on the porch and write. I think we need a porch swing. There are hooks for one. What do you think?"

"I think a porch swing would be really nice. You and I can sit out there, enjoying nature, watching the sunset," Rhys agreed.

"When we go to town, we'll have to see if we can order one." He gave Rhys a kiss. "Thank you for setting up the lawn furniture."

"I think back in the old place I used the patio furniture more than you did. I figured the noises of the city kept you from focusing like you wanted to. This time, I wanted it set up where you would be able to enjoy it as much as I do."

Peter kissed his cheek. "The city noise, the duplex noises, and everything else kept me from concentrating. Thank you for thinking about me when you set it up."

"You should have gotten a picture of it, because it's about the only heavy lifting I plan on doing for the rest of the renovations."

Peter laughed even harder, sliding his arms around Rhys's waist as he gave him a soft kiss on the tip of his nose. "Sorry I missed such an event."

Rhys leaned into Peter's arms, his forehead resting against his. "I love you, baby. Thank you for buying me this house."

"Anything for you, for always and forever."

Chapter 6

PETER SAT in the chair under the tree and brought the table a little closer to set his drink down. He looked around the yard. The trees with their vibrant colors, the chill in the air that made him think of Halloween and pumpkins. A slight breeze stirred, causing a few leaves to fall from the trees. He watched them float toward the ground, amazed that he could actually hear a leaf fall. The leaves drifted down by the handfuls each time the wind blew slightly, and it sounded almost like rain. He hoped the sudden rapid fall of leaves didn't mean winter was coming fast and hard.

Taking a deep, calming breath, he closed his eyes, trying to connect with his story.

"Who's talking to me today?" He began to open each of his many stories. He never worked on just one at a time—he had too many ideas, too many voices demanding to be heard. Sometimes so many bounced in his head that he was lucky if he got a sentence down before moving on to the next. That was the biggest pain in the ass, when the voices in his head refused to take a number and wait in line.

He stared at the house, trying to decide the best way to describe it. He had a story on the edge of his mind, the characters flitting in and out but nothing concrete. Peter knew he wanted to have the house be the center point of the story, though, perhaps the home of a reclusive vampire.

He stared at the house trying to decide how to begin as a gentle breeze blew, rustling the trees. It was nice not to hear the honking of horns, the general noise of people and traffic, to hear the music in silence that most people in the city never heard.

He stared at the lower stories of the house, the porch that wrapped around it, the stone pillars. He loved the fact that the builders seemed to have found rocks and not used the perfectly formed ones that houses had nowadays. It gave the house character, unlike the new houses that all seemed to be the same size, shape, and color. When had we as a nation decided conformity was the way to go and not let our individuality show?

"Pillars crafted of stone, the rock hauled from the bank of the river and worn smooth over the years by the elements," he mumbled to himself. Perhaps he would have a farmer building the house brick by brick and stone by stone for his beautiful new wife. It would be his standing testament to the woman he loved before he goes to war and dies from a gunshot wound never to see his wife or beloved home again. He shook his head. That was too contrived.

He looked at the second floor of the house. It seemed no matter how much he stared at it, the story that was flittering around the edge of his imagination just wasn't coming to light. Writer's block was a rare thing for him. The damn characters came in all shapes and sizes and never seemed to shut up. In the two weeks since moving in, though, his stories just didn't appear as they normally did. He'd spend hours reading and rereading what he wrote, only to add a single paragraph, to change one sentence. He tried to tell himself that the stress of moving into a new house caused it. Once they were settled, the stories would flow. He wasn't so sure, though. Maybe he really didn't have any more stories in him. It scared him a little, not that he would tell Rhys that. He knew what Rhys would say. He would give him that sexy as hell smile and tell him he was trying too damn hard. If he just spent a few days relaxing, the stories would come once again.

Peter tilted his head to one side. He could almost swear someone was in the bedroom window staring down at him. He couldn't see the features clearly, but he knew it was a young man with dark hair. His forehead wrinkled. It was his imagination, his mind making a man out of whatever was really in the window, but it looked so very real. He opened a new document on his computer.

"Go with Demetri, Alexey. He will take you to America, give you a good home, an education we can't provide."

Apprehension settling into his eyes, Alexey looked at Demetri. "I should stay here with you and Papa. Now that he can't work you need me more than ever."

"You go to America, Alexey," his father said. "Hitler's armies have been moving closer. It won't be long before all able-bodied men will be called to duty. I would rather you go to America than risk losing you on the war front."

"I'll tell you what." Demetri smiled at them all. "I'll give Alexey a job. He can keep house for me, cook a little, and just help wherever I need it. In return I will pay for his education and give him a small allowance to send back to you every month. This way he will be getting the education you want for him, and he will be helping you in the way he desires."

Alexey sighed deeply. He didn't trust Demetri, but his parents were right. He would have opportunities in America that he didn't have here. If he became soldier, who knew when, or if, he would get paid. It was better to go to America and be guaranteed a check than to fight and hope for one.

Alexey looked first at his parents, then Demetri. "Fine, I shall go to America, then."

Peter stopped typing. He had no idea where that story came from. It wasn't the kind he normally wrote, not unless Demetri was a werewolf or something along that line. Perhaps it was Alexey that was the shifter, something small and cunning like a fox. He looked back at the house once more. Whatever he thought he saw in the window was gone.

He reread what he wrote once again. He knew he should never edit as he wrote, but it was his one bad habit when it came to writing. Okay, if he was honest with himself, he had a lot of bad habits. He pushed save as the scene that had been flowing well left his thoughts.

Sighing softly, he shook his head and closed his laptop. Perhaps he should just decorate the house for Halloween. He doubted they would get trick-or-treaters out here, but he still loved to decorate for the holiday. He could do it here and not worry about vandals, like he did in the city. It wasn't that they had lived in a bad neighborhood, but pranks got pulled every year in some of the best neighborhoods. He glanced back at the second-story window

"It's a beautiful day, isn't it?" Rhys crossed the yard to stand before him.

"Where did you get the flowers?"

Rhys gestured to the field on the left. "I was just trying to decide what area to clear first. They aren't that pretty, being this late in the season, but I thought they would brighten the kitchen a little."

Peter pulled one from the bouquet and slid it into Rhys's hair as he gave Rhys a quick kiss. "I think the flower makes you look beautiful."

Rhys giggled. He set Peter's computer on the table and straddled Peter.

"Are you feeling a little frisky?" Peter asked, sliding his hands around Rhys's slim waist.

"Just wanted to kiss a little." He leaned forward and rested his forehead against Peter's.

"We're in the country, you know. No one will see us if you get naked."

"Country or not, you know I'm not a big fan of sex outside." He licked the tip of Peter's nose.

"Ick." Peter wiped his wet nose with the back of his hand as Rhys laughed.

He quickly licked the side of Peter's face, laughing harder as Peter reached up to wipe the slobber off.

Peter slid his hands through Rhys's blond hair. He kissed him, tentative at first, lips touching briefly and pulling back slightly before touching again. Peter felt the hot breath against his skin, Rhys's arms around his neck. He touched Rhys's bottom lip with his tongue, a quick dart before pulling back. Rhys moved forward a little. Peter kissed him, darting out his tongue again to touch the bottom lip, trace it, then push into his lover's mouth. Peter could taste the mint Rhys had been sucking on earlier. He began to suck on his full lower lip, his body shuddering as he felt Rhys's hot breath brush over his face.

His cock grew hard, straining against his jeans. He thrust up a little, rubbing against the ass he knew so well. He skimmed his fingers up and down Rhys's sides as Rhys tightened his grip and began to thrust a little.

"Take this off," Peter whispered against Rhys's lips as his fingers found the edge of his shirt.

Rhys pulled back a little so Peter could pull the shirt over his head. Peter began to kiss his neck, sucking slightly, letting his teeth skim along those areas he knew would drive Rhys crazy. He tossed the shirt to the ground beside him as he ran his hands over Rhys's back. He attached his mouth to one nipple, sucking hard and fast like a child searching for milk. Rhys leaned forward, pressing his chest against the sucking lips, his arms tightening around Peter's neck.

Peter reached down and unfastened Rhys's jeans and pulled them open so he could reach Rhys's growing cock. He could feel a damp patch on Rhys's underwear from the precum that leaked at a steady pace. He ran his thumb over the swollen, wet head, making Rhys shudder and arch against him. Peter brought the thumb up to his mouth and sucked the liquid from it, tasting the salty sweetness that was Rhys.

Rhys stood for a moment on shaky legs. He shoved down his jeans and underwear. Peter reached out to take hold of his hard, throbbing cock and stroked it a little, running his thumb in circles over the head as Rhys climbed back on his lap.

"Fuck, baby, keep that up and I'll shoot my load here and now." Rhys dug his fingers into Peter's shoulders.

"Let me get undressed." Peter took hold of Rhys's hands to steady him.

"Not yet." He straddled Peter. "I want to feel the roughness of your clothes against my naked body. I want to feel exposed and naughty while you are fully dressed."

"Really?" Peter chuckled. He gripped the firm, round asscheeks and spread them so his fingers could graze Rhys's hidden hole.

"Hmm." Rhys began to kiss Peter's neck. "This is actually one of my fantasies, you know. I could never be naked in public like this when we lived in the city."

"Well, we could have tried," Peter teased. "I'm not sure Mrs. White would have approved but we could have tried."

Rhys chuckled. "Mrs. White would have probably have taken pictures."

"Let me fulfill your fantasy, then." Peter pulled Rhys close, raising him up so his cock was trapped between their bodies.

Rhys began to dry hump his lover's clothed body. Peter pushed against the tight, hot hole in time with Rhys's thrusts. He didn't push hard enough to enter him, knowing they had no lube and a dry invasion, even if it was a finger, would be a bit painful.

"Fuck, baby, I want you in me." Rhys rubbed himself against the rough denim that encased Peter's hard cock.

"We don't exactly have lube out here."

"I don't care." He unfastened Peter's jeans, reached in, and took hold of Peter's cock, then began to stroke it, using the precum leaking from the tip as lube.

Peter pushed his finger a little way into Rhys's tight hole, hearing him suck in his breath. He stroked Rhys's cock faster, constantly swirling his thumb over the tip to bring more of the precum down the shaft.

"Oh fuck, I can't believe how good this feels."

"The last time you complained about chigger bites."

"Not on the ground," Rhys gasped as Peter buried his face in his neck.

Peter began to suck on Rhys's neck, his teeth gently scraping along the skin. Rhys thrust harder and faster, dry humping Peter, the rough material of Peter's clothing giving him the friction he needed. Peter looped his shirt around Rhys's cock and squeezed it slightly as he used his other hand to play with his hidden hole. Rhys's breath became harder and faster, his thrusting more frantic.

"That's it, baby, come for me," Peter whispered against his skin.

Rhys continued to thrust, a moan escaping his lips. Peter bit at his jawline, his teeth scraping the skin. Rhys threw his head back and screamed as his orgasm rocked his body.

"Well, that was awesome."

"Fucking A." Rhys laid his head against Peter's shoulder, his breath still coming in ragged gasps.

"We really need to do that more often." Peter ran his hands up and down Rhys's back, caressing him. He tilted his head until it rested against Rhys, content to just hold Rhys and to be in his arms.

"Now I feel nude." Rhys chuckled, lifting his head.

"But you're still the hottest thing I ever laid eyes on." Peter kissed his cheek, not wanting to let the man go, but knowing he probably should get dressed. "You're right, though, you should probably get dressed. With our luck, today would be the one day our neighbors decided to stop by and see us."

"Do you think this place has a welcome committee?" Rhys asked as he stood. His hand traveled to his crotch, covering his nakedness.

"Getting shy?" Peter asked, nodding to Rhys's hand. He reached out and touched Rhys's hips, his fingers barely making contact with the skin as Rhys moved around the chair and picked up his clothes.

Rhys looked down to his hand. "Guess it's a natural reaction to being nude and outside." He pulled on his underwear and jeans, then turned back to Peter and leaned down to give him a kiss.

"Do we need to go to town for anything?" Peter asked as Rhys straightened back up. He ran his hand along Rhys's smooth chest, loving the feel of the man.

Rhys pulled his shirt over his head. "I can't think of anything. We do need to make it to the city one of these days, though. I want to get some new shelving, and I couldn't find what I was looking for here."

Peter nodded. "We can head up there this weekend if you want. We can spend the day there, go out to eat, catch a movie."

"Yeah, I can't believe when we looked at this house, I didn't pay more attention to the town. What kind of town doesn't have a movie theater?" Rhys pulled out the second chair and sat down. He automatically reached across the table to take Peter's hand.

Peter laughed, squeezing the long fingers. For as long as Peter could remember, if they were close enough, they held hands or touched in some way. "I don't know, one that has only four thousand people?"

Rhys picked up Peter's empty glass as he stood back up.

"At least we got a kickass house. I guess if we really want to catch a movie, we can drive the twenty-eight miles and see it."

"That's my darling Rhys, never looking at the area around the sparkly." Peter bit his lips to hide his smile.

Rhys placed his hand on Peter's shoulder and gave a slight shove. "You didn't say anything about the town either."

He shrugged. "I've never lived in a small town. I thought it might be fun. You read about how quaint small towns are with their community events. I personally am looking forward to the ice cream socials and parades. It's almost like I've stepped back in time, Rhys. I can go to an honest-to-God ice cream social and write about it. Maybe I have to change it a little to set it in the right era, but it will give me an actual basis to start with. I'm never seen an ice cream social, you know. How about a county fair? This town has one with the homemade pies and jams. I have seen them on TV, and when I write, that is all I have to go by. Can you imagine what it will do to my stories when I can actually put feelings into a story? I mean, I have feelings, but they will be much more intense when I can experience a fair myself."

Rhys snorted. "We really didn't think this through, did we, two gay guys living in small-town mid-America? We could have always driven down here for you to experience that stuff. Instead we buy a house in the middle of nowhere. We're probably the only gay guys around."

"So, gay guy, do you want to drive into town and get something to eat?"

Rhys wrapped his arms around Peter's shoulders. Pulling Peter close he gave him a wet sloppy kiss. "I think we should just go to town, get some Mexican food, bring it home, and watch a movie."

"Ewww." Peter wiped his mouth, closed his computer, and stood up. If Rhys wanted Mexican for lunch, then that's what they would have. He wanted to check out the town anyway, maybe get a few pictures of the buildings. He had a story forming in his head, and this town would be the focal point. "Gay guy slobber, it's like a cootie kiss."

Rhys slapped his ass. "Give me a few moments and I'll be ready to go."

Chapter 7

RHYS CLIMBED the stairs, his hand running over the banister. He stood in his house—he knew it, but somehow it was different. The walls had been painted a muddy-golden color. He wrinkled his nose. It had to be the ugliest color he'd ever seen. He noticed the green carpet that ran down the hallway and wondered who had decorated the house. It had to be a straight couple—no gay man with any self-worth would decorate his house in such god-awful colors. Rhys could hear someone moving around in the bedroom, opening and closing dresser drawers. He sighed softly. It would be nice if Peter put clothes away, but with the sound of the drawers opening rapidly and then slamming shut, it meant Peter was in the room making a mess that Rhys would have to clean up.

"Peter, are you up here? If you are, you better not be making a mess of those drawers. You know how I hate not having things nice and neat."

Rhys walked toward the bedroom expecting to see Peter in front of the drawers or maybe even by the bed. The room was empty. He looked around thinking Peter might have gone into the bathroom.

"I like Peter."

Rhys spun around, his heart beating wildly. Behind him stood a man who looked barely out of his teen years, early twenties maybe. His black hair hung to his shoulder in loose curls, and it looked wet, like he had just gotten out of the shower. His large dark eyes had some of the longest lashes Rhys had ever seen. They had dark marks under them, like the man hadn't slept in a very long time. He was a thin man, slight of build, and he looked like a strong wind would blow him away.

"You like Peter?" Rhys thought that was the oddest thing to say. How did this man know Peter? Was he a fan of his writing, had he seen his picture on the back of a book?

"I want Peter." The man took a step closer to Rhys.

"You want Peter for what?" Rhys was slightly confused.

The man disappeared only to reappear on the other side of the room. Rhys spun around. Something was not right. People didn't disappear and reappear like that.

"You're in my way. Will you leave and let me have Peter? Are you going to continue to be in my way?" The man glared at Rhys as he walked in a slow circle around him.

"You can't have Peter," Rhys stated. "He's married to me."

"I. Want. Peter." The man spoke each word slowly, his tone clipped.

"You. Can't. Have. Peter," Rhys argued, his words just as clipped. "He's mine!"

The boy looked at him for a moment before an evil smile spread across his face. "We shall see."

Rhys jerked awake. He lay there for a moment staring at the ceiling. He'd been having the oddest dream. He didn't have any idea why he would dream someone wanted Peter. They had never had trouble with infidelity. Neither had even looked at another man the entire time they had been together.

He rolled onto his side and snuggled up to Peter, who pulled him closer, murmuring something in his sleep. Rhys always slept better when he was in Peter's arms. He felt safe, loved, protected. He closed his eyes, his hand sliding down until it rested on Peter's stomach. He was just about to drift off when he heard a thump downstairs. His eyes flew open, and he lay still for a moment, trying to decide if something had fallen downstairs or if it was a branch hitting the side of the house. He strained to make out any noise that didn't fit in, but nothing seemed out of place.

He snuggled closer to Peter, getting comfortable, the bridge of his nose pressed firmly against Peter's jaw. It must have been a lingering part of a dream that had woken him up. He closed his eyes, feeling the steady rise and fall of Peter's chest under his hand, and listened to Peter's deep breathing as he slept. He breathed in Peter's scent, a comforting smell that always reminded him of fall and spice. He sighed, telling his mind to sleep, to clear itself of all thought.

Just as he drifted off to sleep once again, he heard a thump, this time from somewhere above him. He rolled onto his back and looked up at the ceiling, trying to decide if he wanted to get up and see whether he'd left a window open in his office. There was a chance a bird might have gotten in. He didn't remember leaving the door that led to the roof open, but if he had, did he really want to see what kind of animal was up there? He would admit he wasn't the manly type of guy. He was more of the hide behind Peter until the danger passed kind of guy.

A thump came from downstairs next, followed by a dragging sound. Heavy footsteps seemed to echo though the house. The soft sounds of muffled crying came from someplace indistinguishable. He rubbed his eyes, fully waking up. He tried to figure out what animal sounded like a crying human when it was trapped. He knew he'd heard of several, but at the moment he couldn't think of what they were. Rhys looked at Peter, trying to decide whether he should wake the man. Peter had been sleeping like crap the last few weeks, and now it seemed he was finally getting a little sleep. Rhys could check out the thumps without waking Peter. It was probably just a tree limb hitting the side of the house. Peter had mentioned a couple needed trimming.

Rhys swung his feet over the bed, shuddering at the cold that seeped into his feet from the wooden floor. He'd heard noises, and he was positive the sounds weren't a lingering effect of the dream. He was going to find out what made the sound and not wake Peter to investigate like he normally would.

"Are you okay?" Peter asked sleepily.

"I thought I heard something. Go back to sleep, and I'll check it out. I probably didn't latch the screen door or something."

"Okay, babe."

As Rhys stood, he felt a hand touch his ankle. Imagining a hand with long pointed nails and dry paper-thin skin stretched tight across the bones creeping out from under the bed, he sucked in his breath and glanced at the floor but saw nothing. He dropped onto all fours. It would be better to turn on the light so he could see under the bed easier, but he didn't want to disturb Peter. He reached forward, gathering up the blankets that hung down so he could see into the dark. It was pitch-black underneath, and he was unable to make out more than vague shapes in the void. Sure he had felt a hand touching his ankle, Rhys leaned in closer. He could almost make out a shape, something under the bed that he couldn't identify. He reached under, trying to grab the odd shape.

"What are you looking for?" Peter's face suddenly appeared on the other side of the bed.

Rhys screamed, falling back against the wall. "You bastard!"

Peter chuckled as he leaned back up on the bed. "You said you were going downstairs, but when I looked over all I saw was your ass in the air. What were you looking for?"

"I thought I felt something touch me," Rhys muttered, looking back under the bed.

Peter looked back under too. "The only thing under here is your jeans. I guess we got a bit wild last night. I do understand how your shirt ended up on the dresser, but I'm not sure how your jeans ended up under the bed."

Rhys shook his head as he stood back up. "I'm still going downstairs to make sure everything is locked up."

"I'm sure it's just the creaks of the house. You know how old houses are. We haven't got enough furniture in it yet to keep the empty hollow sound away." Peter fluffed his pillow a little more before lying back down on it.

"I still wish to check. If I don't, then I'll spend the rest of the night awake wondering about every sound."

"Do you want me to go?"

"No, stay in bed. Keep it warm for me. I need to look myself to ease my mind."

"If you're sure." Peter looked a bit skeptical.

Rhys tried to be brave. He never went to check out sounds by himself. Two things scared Rhys more than anything—thunderstorms and unidentified sounds.

He leaned over to give Peter a quick kiss. "More than sure."

"Hurry back, the bed gets cold without you."

Rhys rolled his eyes as he opened the door. "You're thinking about sex again, aren't you?"

Peter smiled from ear to ear. "Well, you just had your ass in the air, of course I'm thinking about sex."

"Are you really going to let me go downstairs by myself?" Rhys asked, not able to believe Peter would actually let him walk downstairs by himself. There could be demented farmer serial killers down there waiting for him.

Peter threw the blanket off. "I was hoping."

"With that attitude, you can keep hoping for sex too," Rhys grumbled, waiting for Peter to join him.

"Remind me to get a pair of house slippers. These wood floors are a hell of a lot colder than they were in the city."

Rhys chuckled. "We had throw rugs down, and the duplex was smaller and much easier to heat. This house is so big we don't heat all the rooms. I think the cold just sort of seeps in under the doors."

"I love your logic," Peter teased.

"Well, one of us had to get the charming good looks and the other had to get the brains. I chose the brains." Rhys inspected his nails, dismissing Peter's comment.

Peter grabbed the pillow off the bed and smacked Rhys with it.

"Peter!" Rhys grabbed the pillow off the floor. He usually was the first to tell Peter not to throw things in the house, but not tonight. He lobbed the pillow back at Peter, who stood on the other side of the bed laughing at him.

Peter ducked and grabbed the pillow off the floor, but Rhys had run across the room and now held a pillow of his own. Peter swung the pillow and hit Rhys in the chest. Rhys crawled onto the bed, swinging wildly back and forth and landing glancing blow after blow. Peter ducked under the onslaught from the pillow attack, grabbing Rhys around the waist.

"Peter, no fair!" Rhys shrieked, using the pillow to repeatedly smack Peter's chest and arms.

Peter laughed harder, and ducking the onslaught of the pillow, he began to tickle Rhys. Damn! Peter seemed to know each and every one of his ticklish spots. As Rhys tried to block Peter from reaching one spot, Peter moved to the next.

"Stop it, Peter! You know how ticklish I am," Rhys howled. Dropping the pillow, he tried to push Peter off him. When that didn't work, he took a defensive stance and tried to keep Peter from tickling him.

"You got to be faster than that." Peter snorted as he dodged Rhys's grasp and continued to tickle him.

"Come on, Peter, stop it. I heard a noise downstairs. There could be someone robbing us blind, or there could be some mass murderer downstairs getting ready to kill us."

Peter stopped his tickling even though he continued to straddle Rhys. "What kind of sound? Was it the sound of something breaking?"

"It was a thump, maybe a dragging sound. I'm not positive. Oh yes and crying, I'm pretty sure I heard something crying."

Peter climbed off Rhys. "You stay here in bed, and I'll go check it out."

"Fuck that. My luck, it's the crazy inbred farmers who are here to sacrifice us to save the crops. You go downstairs to investigate, find nothing because the crazy ass people are up here killing me."

Peter laughed. "Now who has the overactive imagination? It must be the gamer in you. You know, maybe if you didn't have so many games that were centered on killing people, you wouldn't see mass murderers behind every tree."

Rhys stuck out his tongue as he rolled off the bed. "I'm going with you."

As they walked out into the hallway, Rhys huddled against Peter's back. Peter opened the doors to each of the bedrooms and turned on the light to make sure each one was empty. He switched on the stairway light to illuminate the bottom landing. They crept down, listening for whatever Rhys thought he heard. The steps creaked, making it sound almost like someone was following them. Rhys glanced over his shoulder to assure himself an ax murderer wasn't sneaking up behind him.

"We would have found him if he was behind us, Rhys." Peter chuckled. "We checked the rooms."

"You didn't check behind the shower door," Rhys protested. "The psycho could have been in there."

Peter stopped, turned to face Rhys, and placed a hand on his hip. "Do you want me to go back upstairs and check the shower?"

"Too late now." Rhys rolled his eyes. "He wouldn't be still behind the shower door. He would have moved into one of the rooms we already checked."

Peter turned and, shaking his head, started walking down the steps again.

"Not so fast, Peter." Rhys hurried down the stairs after him.

Peter stopped at the bottom and waited for Rhys. "I want to get the house checked and get back in bed. I swear, you really should warm me up in a really special way after all this."

Rhys rolled his eyes. "You really don't think with anything other than your cock, do you?"

Peter chuckled as he walked into the front room. "Not usually, but you know that after eight years. Look, baby, I love you to no end, but I don't think there is anything here. You heard some animal outside or the house settling or whatever."

"You're probably right. That doesn't mean you're not going to check every room and closet in the house to reassure me," Rhys countered.

Peter sighed softly, turned to face Rhys, and slid his arms around the man's waist. "I'll do it for no other reason than I love you."

"I love you too, baby." Rhys gave him a kiss. "Now hurry up and check the rest of the house. My body is getting cold, and I need someone warm to snuggle up with."

Peter resumed looking through the rest of the house for the unseen noise maker. Rhys stayed pressed against Peter's back as they went from room to room. If someone had been in the house, Rhys knew Peter could not have defended them, not with Rhys almost a second skin.

"There is nothing in the house, Rhys. Can we go back to bed?"

Rhys looked around the kitchen. Everything was in place. "I'm not really tired now."

"Then come to bed. You and I can do something about that."

"Could we go watch TV for a little while?" Rhys asked. "I'm not ready to get back in bed."

Peter looked at him. Rhys had wrapped his arms around his chest as if he could give himself some sort of comfort. Peter pulled Rhys into his arms, giving him the comfort he needed. "It's two in the morning, sweetie. There's nothing on. Come back to bed, baby, and I'll hold you, tell you a story, fuck you through the mattress, whichever appeals to you."

"It all comes back to sex with you." Rhys sighed, glancing out the back window. He chewed on his bottom lip as he tried to decide if Peter needed to check outside.

Peter gave a soft sigh and reached up to grip the Rhys's jaw to turn his head so he could look him in the eyes. "It has nothing to do with sex, Rhys, and everything to do with being tired. Let's just go to bed. You can cuddle in my arms and sleep will come. I promise you that."

Rhys took his hand. "Okay, baby, let's go to bed."

Chapter 8

RHYS LEANED back in his chair, stretching his whole body. He glanced at the clock and was not at all shocked to see he had been working at least four hours on his game. He always lost track of time when he got in the groove. He pushed his chair away from his desk and stood, his whole body protesting the movement. He stretched again, trying to work the kinks out of his neck and back. His stomach growling reminded him that he hadn't eaten yet.

"Might as well take a break." He sighed, saved all his work so far, and turned off his computer.

Rhys closed the door to his office and jogged down the stairs to the second floor. Glancing into Peter's office, he found the room to be empty.

"Must be working outside," he murmured, pulling the office door closed. He walked down the hall and headed down the stairs.

The front room shone brightly. Peter must have opened the curtains to let in the sunlight before he went outside. Looking around the room, he noticed the glass sitting on the table and the paper scattered on the floor. Giving a sigh and a shake of his head, Rhys crossed the room to pick up the paper. He placed it neatly in the magazine rack, grabbed the glass off the table, and headed for the kitchen.

"Hey, babe." Peter looked up as Rhys entered the dining room.

"Peter, how many times have I told you not to leave your dishes sitting in the front room or the paper all over the floor? You didn't even have a coaster under it."

Peter looked at the glass in Rhys's hand. "Sorry."

"So why aren't you in your office writing?"

Peter began to type again. "I couldn't think upstairs. I was going to go outside to write, but I decided to grab some OJ and read the paper instead. I was halfway through the paper when I had a story thought. I had left my laptop on the dining room table, so this is as far as I got."

Rhys shook his head. That was so typical of Peter. He walked around the table, pushed open the kitchen door, and stopped in his tracks. Every door in the kitchen stood open, every drawer and every cabinet. Rhys turned on his heels and walked back into the dining room.

"What were you looking for in the kitchen?" Rhys leaned against the doorframe.

"What do you mean?"

Rhys gestured behind him. "You left the cabinet doors open and all the drawers pulled out."

Peter shook his head, his forehead wrinkling a little in confusion. "I haven't been in the kitchen, Rhys."

"Well, all the cabinet doors are open, and I didn't do it. The last time I checked, only you and I are here so that really narrows down who did it."

Peter slid his chair back and headed for the kitchen. "I haven't been in the kitchen for hours, Rhys. Maybe we need to put some latches on the cabinets. It could be the hinges are loose and the doors just open as the house settles."

"I'd think after two hundred years the house would be settled," Rhys teased him.

Peter opened and closed the door, testing the tightness of the hinges. "When we go to town I'll get new hinges and rehang all the doors. It'll give us a chance to paint them."

"Dark cherrywood?"

Peter shrugged, and pulling Rhys into his arms he gave him a quick kiss. "You know the kitchen is your place. If that's what you want, then that is what we'll do."

"You know I like it when you pull out the tools and get all sweaty." Rhys gave him a quick kiss before stepping away.

Peter laughed. "Then why is it every time I mowed the lawn at the duplex you would tell me to shower before I touched you?"

"Sweaty from doing something all macho and sweaty from working are two different things." Rhys swatted his butt. "You putting on a pair of low-riding jeans, a tool belt, and nothing else will have me hard and attacking your body."

Peter laughed. "Maybe when I hang the cabinet doors, I'll wear the tool belt and nothing else."

Rhys stuck his finger in his mouth and sucked it slightly as he thought about that image. "Nah, let me take something off you—jeans and a tool belt."

Peter took the wet digit from Rhys's mouth and placed it in his own, then sucked slightly. Rhys closed his eyes, moaning and swaying softly.

"Sometimes something so simple can be so erotic," Rhys whispered.

Peter closed his eyes and continued to suck the finger.

"Of course I do have something else that likes to be sucked on too."

"Your neck?" Peter asked.

"Well, I do like to have that sucked also." Rhys tilted his head to one side, indicating that Peter should begin to suck there.

Peter wrapped his arms around Rhys. His lips found Rhys's pulse, and he began to gently suck the area.

"Damn that feels good."

Peter smiled against Rhys's neck as his fingers found the hem of the shirt and then pulled it up. Rhys backed up against the wall, his fingers fisted into Peter's hair as Peter continued to suck on his neck.

"We will never get to town if you do that." Rhys gently pushed him away.

"Town's not that important. We can go anytime." Peter didn't let Rhys get far. He nuzzled his neck once more and ran his tongue along Rhys's pulse, feeling the quick flutter.

"Fuck, you know exactly where to suck." Rhys sighed.

"I know someplace even better." Peter dropped to his knees in front of Rhys.

Rhys ran his hands through Peter's hair, feeling the silky softness, then moved them over his shoulders and back up along the side of his face and into his hair again.

Peter unfastened Rhys's pants. He pulled the fly open, then buried his nose against the bulge. He breathed deeply, smelling the musky man scent. He licked the rough material, feeling the shape of Rhys's penis through the cloth.

"We were going to go to town, Peter," Rhys said with very little conviction.

"Later," Peter mumbled, his teeth scraping at the stiffening rod.

Rhys opened his legs a little wider and fisted his hands in Peter's hair, pulling his head closer to Rhys's crotch as he began to rhythmically thrust.

Peter pulled Rhys's underwear down a little to free his growing cock. The pink tip peeked out, ready for his tongue. Peter smiled and obliged it, his tongue swirling around the spongy tip.

"Fuck, Peter," Rhys gasped.

"Do you want to fuck right here in the dining room, or do you want to take it elsewhere?"

"Here." Rhys managed to straighten up.

Peter yanked Rhys's jeans down in a couple of hard tugs, and Rhys used Peter's shoulder for support as he stepped out of his jeans. Peter smiled at him before he took Rhys's hardening cock back into his mouth. His fingers gripped the slim hips to hold Rhys still so he could suck the cock that was growing harder in his mouth with each tug.

"Oh my God," Rhys whispered, thrusting into Peter's mouth.

Peter pulled away from the thrusting cock. He stood, lifted Rhys, then sat him on the dining room table and stepped between Rhys's legs. Rhys lay back and raised his leg up over Peter's shoulder.

"You're so fucking sexy," Peter whispered, running his hand down Rhys's leg. He stood for a moment using his nails to tease the area, to watch his cock twitch whenever he hit a really ticklish spot.

"Thank you," Rhys moaned, one hand pinching his nipple, the other sliding down into his pubic hair. He began to rhythmically pull at the short blond hair matching the tugs to the pinching of his nipple.

The sight of Rhys pleasuring himself, biting his lip to help contain the groans, made Peter harder than he thought he could ever be. He leaned over and kissed Rhys's stomach. Rhys shifted a little, making himself more comfortable, as Peter began to lick his smooth skin. Peter let his tongue swirl around his belly button occasionally thrusting into the small hole. Rhys took Peter's hand, and pulled it to his mouth to suck on Peter's fingers. Rhys had a wicked smile on his lips, his eyes half closed in lust.

"I want you in me, babe."

"We didn't bring anything down here."

"Fuck!"

"We can still have fun without penetration," Peter reminded him, taking Rhys's cock back in his mouth.

"You're right. I'm going to enjoy this, but are you going to be getting the same enjoyment?"

Peter stopped sucking for a moment so he could answer Rhys. "I get pleasure out of giving you pleasure."

Rhys snorted. "Yeah, I'll buy that. Get back to giving me pleasure."

Peter chuckled. He licked the hard cock, tasting the salty precum. He knew the taste better than anything. He could be given a sample of the salty liquid blindfolded, and he would know it was Rhys's. He continued to suck, taking the cock as far into his mouth as possible. Sometimes he could deep throat Rhys, but not all that often. Even then he could only take Rhys down his throat for a few thrusts before he started to gag.

Peter reached for Rhys's nipples, finding the hard nubs without looking. He began to pull at the little buds, bringing forth a moan from Rhys. Peter twisted the rosebud, causing Rhys to thrust hard into his mouth. Peter sucked, matching Rhys's thrusts. Every time Rhys thrust up, Peter made sure he was plunging down.

"I'm close, Peter!"

Peter tried to suck Rhys down his throat, wanting to have him as deep as possible when he came. He pulled and twisted his nipples knowing how much Rhys liked little bit of nipple pain as he achieved his orgasm.

"Fuck!" Rhys screamed out, shooting deep into Peter's mouth.

Peter pulled Rhys's cock as far down his throat as possible, loving the taste of his lover's cum. He drank it in, sucking hard, hoping to get each and every drop.

"Fuck, baby," Rhys panted, running his hands through Peter's hair.

"I love you, baby, more than anything."

"We can't exactly snuggle on the table," Rhys pointed out.

Peter continued to lie on him, his head on Rhys's stomach.

"Come on, Peter, baby, stand up. If you want we can go upstairs and cuddle, maybe do this again in a little while with actual lube and penetration."

Peter slowly stood. He offered his hand and helped Rhys off the table. Rhys leaned against him, his legs still weak from the orgasm.

"I do love you." Rhys kissed Peter's cheek.

"So how important is a run to town?"

"Fuck it." Rhys snuggled into his arms. "I'll figure supper out with whatever is here. Take me upstairs and claim me again."

Chapter 9

"I'M GLAD you're home, baby." The dark-haired man looked up from where he sat under the tree.

Peter looked around the yard. When had they placed the small bench under the tree? *"I'm dreaming, aren't I?"*

"Dreaming? I'm not sure what you mean by that."

Peter took a good look at the man. His name was Alexey, but Peter wasn't sure how he knew it. Alexey's lip was a bit swollen, his cheek held the faintest traces of a bruise. Peter sat on the small bench beside the small dark-haired man. Alexey really needed a haircut. His bangs were so long they fell into his eyes. *"What happened?"*

"Oh, Peter, you know what a klutz I am. I hit the doorjamb. I'll be fine, though."

Peter ran his thumb over the swollen lips before leaning forward to gently place a kiss on them. *"You need to be more careful, sweetie."*

"I know I need to be. Do you love me?"

Peter pulled Alexey into his arms. He ran his hands down the man's back. Alexey seemed so small, so fragile somehow. *"Of course I love you, Alexey. You know that."*

"Will you protect me? Do you wish to always be with me?"

Peter kissed the top of his head, hugging him just a little tighter. *"What do you need me to protect you from?"*

"Anyone who would hurt me. Would you protect me?"

Peter nodded. *"You need to gain a little weight, baby. You're nothing but skin and bones."*

"You don't think I'm too fat?"

"Never. You're perfect, you know that."

"Make love to me, Peter. Show me how special I am. Show me how much you love me." He pulled at the hem of Peter's shirt, and his fingers skimmed the hot, smooth skin.

"Right here?" Peter looked around. Something bothered him about all this. He just wasn't positive what. He knew it was a dream, but even though he knew it, there was just something so wrong about it.

"Right here, Peter. Right here in the open. Fuck going to the bedroom and being all proper. I want you to show me what it's like to be loved. I want to feel your hands all over me. I want to hear you scream out my name. I want to know I turn you on."

Peter grabbed him around the waist. He stood suddenly and swung the man in a circle, laughing as he did. Alexey laughed, grabbing hold of Peter's shoulders.

"Wrap your legs around my waist, and I'll take you inside."

"No, Peter, not in the house. Make love to me out here in the open," he whispered against Peter's lips between kisses, his legs wrapped tightly around Peter.

"Are you sure?"

He nodded, his forehead pressed against Peter's. *"Right here on the grass. I want to feel nature and you."*

Peter nodded, lowering them both to the ground as he kissed Alexey's neck. Alexey saw Peter lifting the bottom of his shirt and pulled away just enough for Peter to raise it above his head.

"What happened?" Peter stared at Alexey's chest, noticing his ribs seemed way too prominent. Several large bruises marred his otherwise perfect chest.

"It's nothing, Peter. Forget the bruises. I bruise easy, you know that." Alexey reached up to kiss him.

Peter leaned back in to bite Alexey's collarbone as he tossed the shirt on the ground. Peter could feel Alexey's erection through his jeans. He reached down to unzip his pants and pushed them open so he could free Alexey's straining cock. His fingers felt the damp spot on

Alexey's underwear. He reached past the waistband of Alexey's underwear and grabbed hold of his throbbing cock. He gave it a few short strokes as his lips found Alexey's nipple. Alexey fell back onto the ground, opening his whole body for Peter's mouth and hands.

Peter sat for a moment enjoying the sight of Alexey lying on the ground, his hands stretched above his head, his pants open, his cock peeking out from the zipper. Peter moved closer to him and began to trail his fingers up and down the smooth skin of Alexey's chest, causing the man to shudder.

"Tell me you love me," Alexey whispered through half-closed eyes.

"You have a beautiful body," Peter acknowledged, lowering his mouth to the hard nipple. A gentle breeze came up, sending a chill over their bodies. Instinctively Peter moved to shield Alexey from the chill of the air.

"How sweet," Alexey whispered. "Not everyone would protect their lover."

Peter kissed his way down Alexey's chest as the man pushed his jeans down, freeing his cock. Peter moved his hand down to the short black pubic hair. He pulled on it just a little, smiling as Alexey closed his eyes and tilted his head further back. Peter licked along the underside of the shaft, his tongue swirling around the tip, licking at the slit tasting the salty droplets.

"Oh God, Peter!" Alexey cried out, grabbing fistfuls of grass.

Peter continued to pinch and pull at the pert little nipples as he drew the throbbing cock down his throat. Alexey fisted his hands in Peter's hair and began to tug. Peter ran his tongue all over the stiff shaft. From somewhere in the distance, Peter heard the ringing of a phone.

"Ignore it, Peter," Alexey whispered to him. "It's not important. Stay with me."

Peter stopped licking the cock. His fingers absently ran along Alexey's chest as he looked toward the house.

"Peter, don't answer the phone," Alexey ordered.

Peter rested his chin on Alexey's hip bone. "Don't worry, baby. I wouldn't be able to make it to the house before it stopped ringing anyway. I was just thinking we didn't bring any lube out."

Alexey shrugged. "Well, we can use spit, or if you want, you can suck me off, then I'll suck you off. It really doesn't matter to me. All I want is you."

Content to lick the rather nice balls, Peter settled back between Alexey's legs. Alexey placed his leg up on Peter's shoulder, opening up more for the soft tongue. His fingers ran through Peter's hair and over his shoulders as Peter moved from the small round balls to that special place just behind them.

"Oh God, Peter, that's the spot. That's the perfect spot."

Peter chuckled. He dipped his head further down and his tongue found the tight secret hole.

"Oh fuck!" Alexey screamed out. One hand fisted Peter's hair and the other dug into his shoulder. "Oh fuck, I want to come!"

"Then come for me, baby." Peter continued to stab that tight hole with his tongue, getting the whole area wet before pushing his finger in.

"With me, Peter. Please, put it in me so you can come with me."

"We don't have any lube," Peter protested, twisting his finger around in the hole.

"Damn it!" Alexey screamed out as Peter covered his cock with his mouth.

Peter sucked hard, drawing out every last bit of cum as Alexey shot into his mouth.

"Oh, Peter," Alexey sighed as Peter laid his head on his hip. "I wish this moment could last forever. I think I love you more than I've ever loved anyone. I know you would be so good to me."

"Do you want to go inside and finish this?"

Alexey smiled. "Yes, I think I'd like that. I'm pretty sure I'll be hard again by time we get into the house."

Peter stood, then reached down to offer Alexey his hand. As he pulled Alexey to his feet, Peter stumbled backward and began to fall.

Peter awoke with a jerk. He looked around the room as the last traces of his dream faded from his memory. It had been so lifelike. He swore he could taste the faintest traces of Alexey still on his lips.

He rose off the couch and stretched his sore muscles. Although comfortable, it wasn't a place he liked to sleep very often and he was a bit surprised Rhys had let him sleep there. Peter rubbed his hands over his face. It had all been a dream—Alexey, the sex, it had all been a dream. It hadn't felt like a dream, though. It had felt so very real. He could feel the tremble of the man when he touched him, felt his breath on his skin. He had never had a dream where he felt everything so intensely.

Suddenly he heard it—a painful, heartfelt sobbing. It came from somewhere above him. Peter crossed the room and headed for the stairs.

"Rhys?" he called up the stairs. "Are you all right?"

He stopped a moment at the bottom of the steps, waiting for a response. "Rhys?" he called again.

He walked up the stairs, and the sobbing became louder, more intense. He couldn't imagine Rhys ever crying that hard. This wasn't the cry of a man in physical pain, but more the cry of a man who felt something on a much deeper level. It was the cry of a man who'd lost the person he loved, the cry of someone who felt nothing but utter dejection.

"Rhys?" Peter called, heading for the bedroom. He wasn't sure why Rhys was crying so hard, but he'd do something to ease his pain. The sound of sobbing tugged at his heart until all he wanted to do was pull Rhys close and let him know he would always be loved.

"Rhys?" he called, pausing by the open bedroom door. Inside, the room was empty, the sobbing had stopped.

"Rhys?" he asked again, walking around the room.

He looked out the window and saw Rhys in the yard, sitting under the tree in the swing, his laptop open. Peter shook his head. He had been so sure he heard someone in the house. Perhaps he really was working too hard, like Rhys had said.

Peter glanced around the bedroom once more, and the feeling he wasn't alone settled over his skin. He shuddered as a chill passed over his body. Suddenly he didn't want to be alone in the house. It wasn't the feeling of sadness. It was a darker feeling, an angrier feeling. He hurried out of the bedroom and down the hall, every fiber in his body telling him to run, to get the hell out of the house before he saw something he didn't want to see. Peter refused to run. He forced himself to walk calmly, if a little quickly, down the hall. He took the stairs two at a time, then hurried across the front room and through the kitchen.

"Hey, baby." Rhys looked up as Peter came out the back door.

"Hey." Peter sat beside Rhys, the feeling of dread leaving him the moment he walked out of the house. "How's the game coming along?"

Rhys shrugged. "Slowly."

Peter kissed his cheek. "Sorry to hear it."

Rhys closed the computer. "Once I get the whole storyline plotted out, then the rest of the game is simple."

"I didn't mean to disturb you."

Rhys shook his head as he gently pushed the swing. "You didn't. I needed a break. It's a beautiful day, isn't it?"

Peter sat listening to the wind blow through the leaves, and felt it caress his skin. "The house was feeling a little stuffy. You didn't happen to hear crying, did you?"

"Why would I hear crying?"

Peter shook his head. "I thought I heard crying inside. Maybe it was an animal or something."

Rhys looked around. "I haven't heard anything. Do you think there may be some rabbits under the house or in the attic?"

"It was probably just the wind. I've been working just as hard as you have—makes me hear things that aren't there."

"Don't expect me to go looking under the house for a rabbit." Rhys shivered. "I leave that stuff to you."

Peter kissed him. "That's what I love about you. You allow me to be the big strong man."

Rhys stood and stretched, working the kinks out of his shoulder. "I'm glad we decided to move to the country. I love the silence, the smells, and the sounds of nature. I can really relax and get into my story here. I'll have the game designed before I know it."

Peter reached over and took Rhys's hand. "I remember a time when video games didn't have storylines."

"You remember a time when two paddles and a ball was a modern video game."

Peter nodded. "I guess it shows how old I'm getting. Do you know being outside seems to help my writing also? For some reason my writer's block seems to go away when I step outside. I know it sounds odd, but it's almost like a fog has lifted. I guess there is just something about nature. I'm getting all kinds of ideas just sitting under the tree and clearing my mind. I can picture this house being the center of many stories. I'm even thinking of trying a new genre."

Pulling his feet up into the swing, Rhys snuggled beside Peter. He ran his hands through Peter's hair. "You know we're alone out here."

"I could put you on all fours, and then your ass will be in the air." Peter licked the man's chin.

Rhys snorted. "Last time we did that, I had a mosquito bite on my dick. Once again, if we fuck outside, you're on the ground."

Peter eased Rhys backward until he lay on the swing. He slid his hands under Rhys's shirt and felt the soft, warm skin. "I might be willing to risk a chigger bite or two. I'm glad you talked me into getting a house so far out no one can hear you scream."

Rhys laughed. He pulled off his shirt and tossed it on the ground beside him. "I plan on screaming out my passion rather loudly, so you better be good."

"Aren't I always good?"

Rhys snorted. "Not lately."

"Hey, you've had an orgasm," Peter protested.

"Not really good mind-blowing ones. The ones you have given me lately were just a little lackluster. Let's face it, baby, you've been missing the mark sexually."

"Really?"

Rhys stretched out his hands above his head. "Really."

Peter adjusted his weight, causing the swing to move back and forth. "Maybe doing it on the swing isn't the best place in the world."

"This is why I'm telling you that when it comes to the actual event you're on the bottom, and I'll ride you long and hard."

"I promise, this time not only will I hit the mark, but you will see stars."

"So far all I hear are words."

Peter pulled his shirt over his head and tossed it on the ground. He then unfastened his pants and shoved them to the ground until he stood naked before Rhys.

"Ahh, you got naked. Yeah, that's your idea of foreplay all right," Rhys teased.

Peter grabbed Rhys up off the swing, and Rhys automatically locked his legs around Peter's waist. Peter turned around and around in circles, and as Rhys laughed, the images from his dream rushed back to him. Peter did have to admit it felt a little odd to be naked outside, the air caressing the areas that usually never experienced sunlight this way.

"You know being in the country now I might take up nude sunbathing," Rhys commented as Peter set him down on the ground.

"Why are you talking and not getting naked? I want to do some major fucking, let you know that I have the skills that not only will make you see the stars and heaven above, but we could be in the middle of a fucking earthquake and you will never know it."

Rhys walked around the swing, his fingers trailing over the back of it. "I'm not sure I'm interested in sex at this moment."

"But I got naked," Peter protested.

"Did I tell you to get naked?" Rhys stayed out of Peter's reach. "I don't remember telling you to strip. I said *if* we have sex outside you're on the bottom."

"You wanted to have sex outside." Peter pouted.

Rhys laughed as he began to skip toward the house. "I think you should go ahead and work on that nude sunbathing."

"Some romantic husband you are," Peter called after the retreating figure as he grabbed up his clothes.

"Typical man. Someone mentions sex and you strip," Rhys called over his shoulder.

Peter slid on his jeans, zipped them up, and headed toward the house. "Hey, Rhys?"

Rhys stopped on the porch. "What baby?"

"Have I told you today that I love you?"

The clear sound of Rhys's laughter was enough to make Peter smile. He began to jog toward the house, wanting to be with his husband. Peter noticed something moving out of the corner of his eye, a shadow that disappeared around the corner of the house.

"Hello?" Peter called, changing direction and hoping to intercept what he thought he saw. He rounded the corner of the house, but nothing was there. He stopped and turned in a full circle, sure what he'd seen wasn't an animal. In fact it almost looked like a small dark-haired man. Shaking his head and giving a soft sigh, he turned back toward the porch.

"Are you coming in?" Rhys stepped back on the porch.

Peter jogged up the steps. "I thought I saw something. It must have been a cloud passing over the sun or something."

"A cloud passing over the sun?" Rhys asked, one eyebrow cocked.

Peter gave him a quick kiss as he passed him. "Thanks for holding the door, baby."

Rhys shrugged. "I figured it was the least I could do. Do you want me to fix you something to eat?"

Peter shook his head. "I'm good but thanks anyway. I think I'm going to read for a little while. Maybe that will help me get past this writer's block I'm having."

"Okay, sweetie, I think I'll put a roast in the Crock-Pot and let it cook since I'm not hungry either." Rhys turned toward the cabinet and pulled the Crock-Pot from its spot.

"No celery, baby. You know I hate celery."

Rhys chuckled. "Surprising how after eight years I remember little things like that."

Peter opened the refrigerator and handed Rhys the roast before he grabbed a bottle of water for himself.

"You better use a coaster if you plan on taking that in the front room." Rhys nodded toward the bottle of water as he took the roast from Peter.

Peter rolled his eyes. "Of course I'll use a coaster."

"Peter." Rhys gave a warning glare.

Peter smiled at him as he pushed the kitchen door open. "I promise, sweetie. I'll put a coaster under the bottle. I know how you get when you see water rings on the furniture."

"And yet you still fail to use a coaster." Rhys sighed.

Peter blew him a kiss before heading into the front room.

Chapter 10

RHYS TURNED on the stereo, and music suddenly filled the room. He turned to look at Peter, and he began to sway his hips, a sexy as hell smile on his lips. Peter saluted him with a wineglass. Rhys turned a slow seductive circle, his arms going above his head, careful not to spill the wine. The move stretched his body out, allowing Peter to catch a slight glimpse of Rhys's stomach.

"Damn, you're hot, baby," Peter called to him.

"Like my ass?" Rhys teased, wiggling it back and forth in front of Peter.

"Come a little closer and I'll slap it."

Rhys smiled and moved quickly out of Peter's reach. Setting his wineglass on the table, he started to unbutton his shirt.

"Oh yes, baby, strip for me."

Rhys opened his shirt and moved his shoulders to flash one side of his chest, and then he closed the shirt before flashing the other side. He turned his back to Peter, and his shirt dropped to show a shoulder, which he rolled before pulling the shirt back up.

"I love you, Rhys."

"I love you too, darling." Rhys slid his shirt off and tossed it at Peter. It landed in a heap on the floor. He continued to dance, his hands going to the fly of his jeans.

A sharp, cold wind blew past them, causing Rhys to stop dancing and Peter to look for an open window. Above them in the hallway, something loudly crashed to the ground.

"What was that?" Peter asked.

Rhys shook his head, grabbing his shirt from the floor. "An animal? Do you think one got in the attic or something? The gust of wind, we must have left a window open and an animal got in."

"We don't leave the door to the attic open, Rhys, and that was a crash in the hallway." He began to head to the stairs. "As for the windows, why would we have such a great gust of air suddenly blow through? The night is clear and still."

"Wait a moment." Rhys grabbed his hand. "We need some sort of weapon."

Peter stared at him. "What do you suggest?"

He shrugged. "If it's an animal, then it might come after us. We need something. How about the broom?"

"I can see it now. There's going to be a raccoon upstairs, and I'm going to beat it with a broom."

"Let me go get a rolling pin or something." Rhys stated. "If it jumps you, I can beat it."

"If it jumps me, you'll scream and run," Peter retorted dryly. "Forget getting a weapon."

They made their way up the stairs, Rhys pressed behind Peter, his hand on Peter's back. Peter reached out and flipped on the light in the hallway.

"My favorite vase!" Rhys forgot all about his fear as he rushed past Peter.

"Glad you're worried about intruders," Peter mumbled under his breath.

"I loved that vase, Peter. You bought it for me on our third anniversary. If there's a freaking animal in here, I'm going to fucking beat it to death with your broom for breaking my vase." He swung the first door open.

They looked around the room. The windows were closed and the room empty. They stepped back into the hallway and moved to the next room. After switching on the light, they found that room also empty and the windows closed.

"There has to be a reason that vase fell, and when I find that reason, it's so dead."

"Do you think it had anything to do with that gust of wind we felt?"

Rhys turned to look at Peter. "Do you really think the gust of wind we felt was strong enough to blow over the vase?"

Peter shrugged. "Fine, it was the ghost."

Rhys rolled his eyes. Shaking his head, he checked the bathroom. "I think being in the country has spooked you, Peter. You've been hearing things since the day we moved in."

"Can you tell me you haven't heard anything?"

Rhys headed back down the stairs. "Of course. All old houses have sounds, but that's all it is, the creaks and moans of an old house."

Peter was about to answer when the water in the bathroom sink turned on, causing them both to jump.

"Old plumbing," Rhys muttered, walking into the bathroom to turn the faucet off. Suddenly the water came on in the shower, the stream blasting against the back wall, and the room quickly steamed up. "I'll call a plumber first thing tomorrow."

"No, it's probably just a leaky washer or something. I can take apart the faucet tomorrow and see." Peter reached in to turn off the water.

"Once again, I love a man who can use his hands." Rhys slid his hand into Peter's back pocket and gave his ass a squeeze.

"I love a man who thinks I'm big and tough." He leaned in to give Rhys a kiss, when a door slammed down the hallway. "What the fuck!"

Rhys stuck his head out of the bathroom. A second door slammed shut, then a third. Downstairs, they could hear more doors shutting and windows rattling.

"Do you hear that?" Peter asked.

"I hear what sounds like doors shutting and windows rattling," Rhys offered, wondering why Peter would ask such a stupid question.

Peter shook his head. "Voices, I think I hear voices."

"Call the cops, Peter. Tell them someone is in our house."

Peter reached for his cell phone. "You call the cops. I'm going downstairs and see who the hell is in our house."

"The fuck you are." Rhys grabbed his arm and pulled him into the bathroom. "We're hiding out while I call the cops."

"Don't you hear the voices, Rhys?" Peter asked again, pulling free of Rhys.

"No, I don't hear voices. Peter, stay here." Rhys slammed the phone shut, forgetting about calling the police as he ran after Peter.

Peter made his way down the stairs, wishing he had remembered to grab the broom. He heard voices, though, he was positive about that. He couldn't make out what was being said, but two people were talking. He instinctively held his breath as if that would make the voices clearer. One voice sounded angry and the other was softer, fainter, almost as if he was pleading for something. Perhaps they had just discovered people were in the house and one of the would-be robbers was angry that the other didn't scout the house better.

Peter glanced around the living room. The voices came from off to his left, louder now but the words still unclear. He moved across the living room, searching for the sound of the voices, each step he took carefully calculated so he wouldn't step on one of the boards he knew squeaked.

"Peter, let's call the cops," Rhys pleaded, pulling on his arm.

"I told you to stay upstairs and call the cops while I investigated. You chose to come with me," Peter reminded him. "Now hush or you'll give away the element of surprise."

Rhys snorted as he moved closer to Peter. "I think they pretty much surprised us when they decided to break into our house."

Peter held up his hand as he approached the dining room. The words were angrier, more clipped. Peter wrinkled his forehead. He could hear the rise and fall of sentences but the words still eluded him. If he could just get a little closer, maybe he could make out what was being said. He peeked around the doorway trying to see if the dining room was clear. He was certain the voices were coming from the kitchen.

"You have to hear the voices now." Peter turned to look at Rhys.

"I don't hear voices, Peter. I think whoever was in the house has left. Maybe they realized someone lived here and got spooked. It was probably some teenagers wanting to make out."

"I hear voices." Peter moved closer to the kitchen. "They're still there."

"Are you okay?" Rhys reached out to touch his forehead, a look of concern on his face. "Are you coming down with something? Has the stress of the move and the deadlines become too much for you? We can get the deadlines pushed back if you want, Peter."

"There are voices, Rhys," Peter insisted. "Fuck this, I'm just going in."

"Peter!" Rhys grabbed for him, but Peter had moved out of his reach.

Peter walked toward the door with more courage than he actually felt. He would show Rhys someone was in the kitchen, two people to be exact. He moved toward the swinging door, intending to shove his way through and demand to know why these people were in his house. He stopped before the door, taking a deep breath to gather his courage.

As Peter reached for the door, it swung toward him. The sudden movement caused him to cry out as a cold wind rushed past him. For a moment, he could almost swear the wind rushed through him, and he could feel this coldness that went to his bones in a way he couldn't explain to Rhys. His hair flew around him, as if he was caught by a sudden gust of gale. He turned to Rhys. The man was plastered against the wall, his eyes wide and his hand on his chest.

"Did you see that?" Peter asked him. "Are you all right, Rhys?"

"I saw the wind blow open the door, and you scream like the devil himself grabbed you. You fucking scared the shit out of me, Peter."

"The wind?" Peter looked at him. "It wasn't just the wind."

Rhys regained his composure. "It was the wind, Peter. Whoever broke into the house realized someone lives here and left."

Peter pushed open the kitchen door. He looked around the kitchen and noticed the back door stood open.

"See, Peter. It was a couple of teenagers who hoped to make out in the old abandoned house." Rhys walked over and shut the door.

Peter shook his head softly. "I guess you could be right."

Rhys locked the door. "We just have to remember to lock the doors from now on. I'm sure whoever it was will go back to town and tell everyone that people live in the house. The road will probably get busy for a few days as people drive by to see if it's true or if the house and its ghost spooked some kids."

Peter ran his hands though his hair, he looked around the empty kitchen. Nothing had been disturbed. As far as he could tell, other than the back door standing open, the kitchen was exactly as it had been after they cleaned up following supper. If someone broke in, wouldn't something have been moved, disturbed in some way?

"Come on Peter, let's go back in the other room." Rhys took his hand and pulled him back out of the kitchen.

"Do you think I'm crazy?"

"No, sweetie." Rhys patted his hand. "You probably heard a car radio or something."

"A car radio?" Peter stopped, yanking his hand from Rhys's grasp. "I heard voices, Rhys. I don't think they were English voices, but I heard voices all the same."

"Peter." Rhys reached for him. "You've been under a lot of stress. It has taken a lot more than expected to get this house the way we want it. With the renovations, you working on final edits, and my game only half-done, we are both getting a little tired and stressed."

"Don't fucking patronize me. I heard voices, not some fucking car radio!" He glared at Rhys.

"Fine, you heard voices. Whoever broke into the house was in the kitchen talking in a foreign language. They heard you coming and took off out the back door."

"Why break into the house? It isn't like we don't have lights on. We have your car parked out by the back door. If someone was going to break in, they had to be complete fucking idiots to not notice someone lived here."

"So what do you think it was?"

Peter rubbed his face hard with his hands. "I think we bought a fucking haunted house."

Rhys rolled his eyes and shook his head. "A haunted house?"

Peter shoved his way past Rhys as he stormed into the front room.

"Come on, Peter. Just think about what you're saying." Rhys followed him.

Peter stopped suddenly, almost causing Rhys to bump into him. "Why is it so hard for you to believe that the house could be haunted?"

Rhys took hold of Peter's waist. "It's not that I don't believe you, Peter."

"It sounds that way to me."

Rhys leaned against Peter, his forehead resting against Peter's. "I think people blame ghosts for everything. Most of the time there is a very real explanation for what you think you see and hear. Maybe it is my video game designer's analytical brain speaking, but I just don't believe our house is haunted."

"What do you think it is, then?" Peter sighed, his arms going around Rhys. He wanted Rhys to make everything right. Rhys always made things better when Peter was stressed, but not this time.

"I don't know what you think you see or hear." Rhys kissed him. "But before we start blaming the unseen, I think we first must rule everything else out."

Peter stepped out of Rhys's embrace. "Maybe you're right. Maybe it is my writer's imagination making something out of nothing."

"I didn't mean it to sound exactly like that." Rhys grabbed for him, but Peter moved out of his reach.

"No, you're right." Peter sighed, walking into the front room. "Why believe in ghosts? I've never lived in the country, and what I'm hearing is nothing more than an old house and the sounds of nature."

"Peter"—Rhys followed him into the front room—"don't be like that."

"No." He flopped down on the couch. "I'm tired, I haven't been sleeping for shit. I have three stories half-written. I have one that is getting ready to go to the line editor. I have to think about going to a couple of conventions and getting everything ready for those. It was the wrong time for us to buy a house. I'm not saying I'm not glad we did it. After all, the price was great, too great actually. Maybe we should have done a little research into the house."

Rhys sat on the coffee table in front of him. He rubbed Peter's knees. "Would it have changed your mind? I wanted this house, and in some way so did you, or we wouldn't be here, Peter."

Peter leaned his head back against the couch, his eyes closed. "You're right, I know it."

Rhys moved to sit on the couch beside him. "Of course I am. You know your life is always much simpler when you just admit I'm right."

Peter chuckled. "You would think I'd remember that."

"Have I told you how much I love you?" Rhys wrapped his arms around Peter's shoulder, and rested his head in the crook of Peter's neck, his knee resting on Peter's thighs.

"You love your husband?" Peter teased. "What a novel thought."

Rhys smiled against him. "After all this time, I still love you as much as I did the day we made the commitment to each other, maybe more."

Peter leaned into Rhys. "I love you more than anything and anyone, my beloved spouse."

"One of these days we should get around to expanding our family."

"Do you want to bring a third person in? I thought you said no to the threesome," Peter teased him.

Rhys smacked his chest. "I'm talking about a child, you idiot."

Peter moved out of Rhys's arms. He rose off the couch and went to look out the windows of the french door. "I'm not positive I'm ready to have a child."

Rhys crossed his arms over his chest. They had discussed this before. "I'm ready, Peter. We aren't getting any younger, you know."

"I don't like to think I'm getting older either," he teased, turning to look over his shoulder at Rhys.

"It's a big step, but we now have a house in the country with a large yard. We have extra bedrooms, and we both work from home. I'm not saying to go and get one now. I'm saying that we now have the means and room for a child. I'm asking you to think about it, Peter. I mean really think about it, as in maybe in the next year we can look into adopting. Think about it." Rhys stood up. He took a few steps toward Peter as he spoke.

"Couldn't you be just as happy with a dog?" Peter tried, turning to look at Rhys.

Rhys rolled his eyes. With an exasperated sigh, he walked from the room. Peter turned back to the window and looked out at the yard. He knew Rhys wanted a child, and perhaps in a way he did too. Certain times of the year a child would be nice, usually around the holidays. A child would change everything for them, though, and he wasn't sure he was ready for that change. He was still a child himself. Okay, if he had to admit it, he was thirty-five, an age when a man should be thinking about a family. It really wasn't that he didn't want kids. It was just something that scared the hell out of him. He was barely responsible enough to take care of himself, let alone another life. Rhys always said he would lose his head if it wasn't attached. He was a scatterbrain, and he knew it.

Peter stared out at the yard. He could almost picture a child running through the yard, and hear the squeals of laughter as Rhys swung him around. He looked closer at the large tree that stood in the yard as he saw something streak by. It almost looked like a man running, but it was gone as soon as it appeared. He stepped back from the windows. Maybe he had seen Rhys's shadow move across the window.

He heard the bedroom door slam. He hadn't thought Rhys was that mad.

"Hey, baby? I didn't mean to upset you." He turned away from the french doors and started across the front room. "I'm willing to think about it. It was just a lot to spring on me."

He heard a second door slam. He thought it might have been the bathroom. Rhys must have really gotten pissed. He jogged up the stairs. "Rhys, baby, I'm sorry."

Peter stood at the top of the stairs. All the doors were open. Maybe Rhys was right, and he was really overworked, hearing and seeing things that weren't there. He shook his head. He was going to have to see a shrink; he was growing surer of that each day. "Rhys?"

"What, Peter?" Rhys called up the stairs.

"Did you just slam a door?" Peter asked, looking in the bathroom to assure himself no one was there.

"Ow! Fuck."

"Are you okay?" Peter hurried to the top of the stairs.

"Yeah, I just spilled my coffee." Rhys smiled up at him. "Bet that surprises you, doesn't it?"

"That you spilled your coffee? Not really. You do get distracted easily at times." He smiled down at Rhys.

"It must have been a muscle spasm, because my arm suddenly jerked, spilling my coffee down the front of my shirt. I'm happy I wasn't wearing a good one."

Peter started back down the stairs. "Perhaps I should help you take it off."

Rhys laughed as he headed back toward the kitchen. "I think I'll be fine. Let me take this off and rinse out the spot."

"You may be right, Rhys. I'm overstressed. Hell, I thought I heard doors slamming upstairs, but every one of them was open."

"I didn't hear the doors slam," Rhys called from the kitchen. "Maybe it was a branch hitting the side of the house or something."

Peter followed Rhys into the kitchen. "Maybe. It just sounded so loud. Remind me later to check the trees to see if one of them needs to be trimmed."

Rhys held up the shirt, looking at the spot on it. He stuck it back under the running water and continued to scrub the coffee stain. "We should probably call someone out to prune the trees by the house anyway."

Peter slid his arms around Rhys, his cheek resting against the man's bare skin. "You feel a little cool. Do you want me to run upstairs and grab you a shirt?"

Rhys turned off the water. "It's okay. I finished laundry, so I have a couple of shirts hanging up in the other room."

Peter took a step back, giving Rhys room to move. Rhys opened the small door and stepped into the room just off the kitchen. It wasn't a very big room. Peter and Rhys couldn't fit in it together, but Peter rarely did laundry anyway.

"We need to talk about landscaping at some point." Rhys tossed his shirt in the washing machine, grabbed a shirt off the hanger, and slipped it on. "Are we wanting to put shrubs by the house or flowers?"

Peter leaned against the doorjamb. "Whatever you want. I personally think maybe putting shrubs on the corners and flowers in between would look nice."

Rhys nodded as he thought about what Peter said. "You're probably right. We should hire a landscaper to take care of the yard. I have no idea how to do any of that stuff. I hate getting dirty, and I don't know what plants and flowers will grow here easily."

Peter chuckled. "I'll call someone tomorrow, all right?"

"I love you, baby. Why don't you go upstairs and see if you can find anything on the house or on this Demetri that we bought it from. You know they say you can find anything on the Internet."

Peter nodded. "I had thought about going into town and looking at the library. Maybe there is something in the archived papers."

"What would you be looking for?" Rhys wanted to know.

Peter shrugged. "Just anything pertaining to the house."

"So let's go into town now."

"Are you trying to humor me?"

Rhys shook his head. "I may not believe the house is haunted but I do agree we need to find out why Demetri never wanted the house sold. Who knows what we will find in the old papers."

Peter gave him a kiss, a large smile on his face. "Great, let me grab a notebook and I'll be ready to go."

Chapter 11

"HAVE YOU found anything yet?" Rhys asked.

"Nothing, no mention of deaths, murders, suicides. Maybe it's all in our heads."

Rhys loaded the next film. "We'll find something."

"Can I help you two?" the librarian asked.

Peter glanced at Rhys. The librarian was eighty, if she was a day. "We were looking for a little information on the house we live in."

"Well, I've lived here all my life. Which house do you live in?"

"721 Missouri Road. It's the large two-story house—"

"With the wraparound porch and widow's walk on top," she finished for him. "I'm glad someone has finally moved in there."

"Do you know if there have been any deaths there?"

Her forehead wrinkled as she thought about it. "Not that I can recall. It's a beautiful house. I'm so happy young people have moved into it and are able to take care of it like it needs to be."

"The realtor said it's been empty for a while now."

"It's only been empty about two years now. There have been a couple of people who rented it, but they never stay. They all are families from the city who just aren't ready for country life. I'm sure it is pretty outdated. It happens when the homeowner becomes too old to really care for the house."

"Do you know anything about the previous owner?" Peter wanted to know.

"Demetri Romanov." She smiled. "He was a very dashing man in his younger years. A Russian art dealer, if I remember correctly, but that was before the Second World War broke out. He moved away for a while. The town assumed he was trying to get his family out of Europe. When he returned in the late fifties, he was a different man than he had been. As the years went by and he grew older, he became a bit of a recluse, never leaving the house and never allowing anyone to come in. He would have his groceries delivered to him but demanded that they be left on the front porch, cash for the delivery was always in the mailbox.

"Sometime in the late eighties he moved into a retirement home. He lived out his final years there, never again stepping foot in his house. He left the house to one of his lifelong friends—his name slips my mind at the moment. He modernized it back in the early '90s, hoping to at least rent it out. It seems that Demetri had a stipulation in his will that the house couldn't be sold. Of course, now that he has been dead for a long while, they were able to overturn the will. I'm glad someone will bring new life to the house. You know, houses need people. They are so sad when they are abandoned."

"Was Demetri married? Did he have any brothers or family?" Rhys asked.

"I don't remember anyone saying he had family, and for as long as I can remember, no one came to visit him. He lived there on his own, and even then, his job often took him away for months at a time, so often the house sat empty."

"That's really kind of sad." Rhys glanced at Peter.

"What about an Alexey?" Peter wanted to know. "What happened to him?"

She shook her head. "As far as I can remember, Demetri always lived alone. There were a lot of women who tried to catch his eye, but he never returned their affections."

"Was there ever an Alexey in the house?" Rhys tried.

She thought about it for a moment. "I was young when Demetri lived there. I can't remember anyone before him, and I am certain there has been no one named Alexey afterward. A young couple from the city moved in, but they didn't stay long. I'm not even sure when they left, just one day the sign appeared on the yard again. Most of us in town just assumed that the house was more work than they wanted to do and with them being so far from the city."

"Have you ever heard of an Alexey living in town, maybe visiting someone?"

She shook her head. "Why the interest in Alexey? Do you have a last name?"

Peter shook his head trying to quickly think of a plausible explanation for his questions. "We found a few pictures and books in the attic, and they had the name Alexey on them. I wanted to make sure either Alexey or his family got them."

"I really wish I could have been of more help, but for the life of me, I can't remember anyone named Alexey living there. Perhaps they were books picked up at a yard sale or something. Like I said, though, no one has stayed in the house since Demetri passed away. I can't say that anyone has ever said why. It's not like they run screaming from the place because it's haunted."

"Could it be haunted?" Peter asked. "I mean, has anyone mentioned ghosts?"

She laughed. "Demetri lived in that house for a good sixty years, so I'm pretty sure the house isn't haunted."

Rhys offered his hand. "Thank you so very much for your time."

Peter stood also. "I'm a writer, so maybe someday if you have time, I would love to hear all you know about the house. I'm thinking of featuring it in a book."

"A writer? How fascinating. What type of books do you write? Maybe we have one of them in our library."

"I write a little bit of everything actually, but I tend to specialize in paranormal romance and horror. My name is Peter McNeil."

"McNeil, you know I think we might have one or two in the library. Didn't you write the book about the haunted hotel?"

Peter blushed slightly. "Yes, I did. The Overland series."

"Maybe some evening you could give an author's talk here in the library? Give your fans a chance to meet you and aspiring writers a chance to ask questions."

Peter glanced at Rhys, who was suddenly interested in the outdated painting on the wall.

"I've got some deadlines coming up, but sure, I'll see when I'm free."

"Oh, the town will be so excited to know we have an honest-to-goodness writer living here. The library has been trying to introduce a series of speakers to the public, but no one wants to come to small-town mid-America. You may be just what we need to entice others to speak about their work." She scribbled her name and number on a piece of paper.

"It'll be my pleasure. Rhys and I moved here to get away from the impersonal city life and become part of a community. You know that Rhys designs video games? His last one, *Dishonored Aftermath*, was number one for more than two months. Perhaps he could speak after me?"

Rhys shot him a look, and if looks could have killed, Peter would be dead.

"Oh I'm just so excited." She squeezed his hand before turning to look at Rhys. "Two famous people moving into our little town. You let me know if you need any research help. I'll be more than willing to help you any way I can."

Peter held up the number as Rhys pulled him from the library. "I'll talk to you real soon. You can count on it."

"Why did you just commit me to a social engagement, Peter? You know I like talking in front of people about as well as I like getting my testicles cut off with a dull butter knife."

"Sounds somewhat painful. I didn't know you had your testicles cut off with a dull butter knife before." He glanced down at Rhys's crotch. "I must admit they've been reattached rather well."

"Fuck you." Rhys pulled his keys out of his pocket. "You know exactly what I mean."

Peter looked at Rhys over the top of the car. "It won't be that bad, Rhys. A bunch of kids who play the game will find it really cool that they can meet you. This is a small town. We need to make friends in order to fit in, and this is the way you do it."

"I don't want to fucking fit in," Rhys grumbled, getting into the driver's side. "I want to be left alone to make video games, to just be us as a couple with no intrusions."

"That's what we were in the city, Rhys, a couple with very few friends and almost no intrusions. You fell in love with a house in the middle of the freaking country. How many people does this town have anyway? Four thousand people tops? We are a part of this community whether we like it or not."

Rhys came to a stop at the only stoplight in town. "Do you want to stop and grab something from the diner while we are in town?"

"Yeah, that's fine, unless you want to cook."

Rhys made a left when the light turned green. He headed down the two-lane street to the small diner. "So we're back to square one."

"Not really. We know that Demetri lived in the house. I just have to figure out how Alexey fits into it all."

"As far as anyone knows, no one named Alexey ever lived in the house." Rhys pulled into the parking lot.

"Maybe Alexey never left the house. I would guess that very few people saw Alexey, and if he used any of the farm to grow food, there would be no reason for Alexey to ever leave."

Rhys climbed out of the car. "I guess. I just think that people would have known about Alexey."

Peter followed Rhys into the diner. "We know Demetri was there, so at least that part of the dream was right. There is a good chance Alexey never left the house."

"Two please." Rhys smiled at the waitress as she appeared.

Peter sat at the table across from Rhys. "Just water."

"You could be right, but on the other hand, if Alexey was killed in the house, why was his death not reported? Wouldn't you would find that information in the paper?"

Peter shrugged.

"My analytical gamer brain is just having problems admitting that our house is haunted by someone who no one knew existed," Rhys said as he glanced at the menu.

"Maybe that's the problem. He died and no one knew he even lived. I know if you killed me, I'd be pretty pissed."

Rhys shook his head. "You would haunt me until I died too."

"Are you two ready to order?"

"I'll take the two-piece chicken dinner with the fries," Rhys placed his order.

"Grilled chicken salad, ranch dressing." Peter closed the menu and handed it back to the waitress.

"So you think the house is haunted by Alexey because he wants people to know he lived?"

Peter nodded. "It's as good an explanation as any."

"I still have problems believing no one knew he existed. Someone had to know he lived and reported him missing when he stopped showing up."

"Didn't she say Demetri traveled back and forth between here and Europe?" Peter asked as the waitress set his salad in front of him. "What if Alexey was European? His family thought he was here in America leading a good life. There was a war after all, people lost contact with each other. If people saw Alexey, Demetri could have told them he was a cousin visiting from Europe. If Alexey didn't speak English, then he wouldn't have gone to town very often."

Rhys chewed thoughtfully on a french fry. "You could be right."

"That explanation suits your analytical brain?" Peter teased.

Rhys shook his head. "Not fully, but it is a place for us to start."

Chapter 12

"HAVE YOU thought about what your editor said?" Rhys asked, snuggling Peter, his head on Peter's shoulder.

"I always think about what Vickie says. Which thing am I supposed to be thinking about?"

Rhys ran his hand up and down Peter's chest. "Adding more bondage to your books."

Peter sighed. He pulled Rhys a little closer, his arm more firmly around him. "I bought a few books on bondage. I got one on submissive roles, but let's face it, I don't think I can write something like that."

"Maybe we need to try some of the things in the book," Rhys offered. "Did you bring them to the bedroom with you?

Peter chuckled. "No, they're in my office. You're right, though. You should read the book. I can't believe some of the things I was reading."

Rhys slid his hand down lower until he was stroking Peter's cock. "Well, it will be difficult, but if you wish, I could tie you to the bed and teach you all about obedience."

Peter began to laugh. "I don't think that's necessary."

"It'll be the best way for you to get accurate descriptions down. How can you describe what it feels like to be tied up and spanked if I don't do it to you?" Rhys asked innocently.

Peter shook his head, rolling his eyes at Rhys's statement. "Since I always cast myself as the hero, I think that I'd have to tie you up so I can accurately describe your reactions."

Rhys rolled onto his back. "You know, since moving into this house, I have become horny as hell. I think I've had more sex in the last month then I've had in the last year."

Peter rolled onto his side and ran his finger in small circles around Rhys's nipples as he watched them grow hard. "You notice I haven't complained about that fact either."

"That is because you, on the other hand, have always been ready to go at the drop of a hat." Rhys smiled at him.

Peter began to slowly kiss Rhys's bare chest, his teeth scraping the skin, his nails skimming Rhys's side in a way that made the man shudder.

"I think my favorite part of your body is your stomach," Peter commented, then thrust his tongue into Rhys's belly button.

"I better make sure I don't get much of a potbelly, then."

Peter gently blew on the wet skin, making Rhys laugh. "I wouldn't mind if you gained weight. It would still be my favorite part of your body. There would just be more of you to love. I think you need to get a tattoo across your stomach that says I belong to Peter."

Rhys ran his fingers through Peter's hair. "Right after you get one that says property of Rhys."

Peter gave a growl as his teeth scraped across Rhys's abdomen, and he pulled down Rhys's boxers and let his cock spring to life. He smiled up at Rhys, his nails now skimming over the newly exposed flesh.

"Suck me, baby." Rhys smiled back.

"I plan on it." He flicked his tongue over the tip. He blew on the leaking slit, making Rhys moan in pleasure. Peter licked along the underside of the shaft. A long slow lick that started at the base, swirled around the tip and back down again. He licked the heavy balls, his tongue lifting one then the other. His long fingers massaged Rhys's thighs, kneading the muscles, relaxing the man more than he already was. Peter continued his strokes, up the underside of the shaft, swirling the tip, and back down, not taking Rhys in his mouth no matter how much Rhys thrust up.

"You seem to be having problems understanding English. I said suck me."

"But then the magic would be over way too soon." Peter smiled. He began to gently blow on the wet skin, making Rhys suck his breath in through his teeth.

Rhys gave a frustrated groan as he tried to thrust his cock into Peter's mouth. He grabbed Peter's head, trying to hold him still so he could thrust his cock in, yet Peter still evaded him

"Don't make me tie you to the bed," Peter warned.

Rhys chuckled. "I don't think you would even begin to know how to tie me to the bed. You don't have a dominating bone in your body."

"I don't know, now that I'm putting some S and M in my stories I may be getting the urge to walk a little on the wild side. After all, how will I know if I'm writing it right if I don't try the shit out on you?"

Rhys threw his hands over his head. "Go ahead, baby, tie me up and dominate me."

Peter stared at him for a moment, trying to decide if he actually could tie Rhys up. He could use a tie or something. He wasn't even sure if they had anything he could use to tie Rhys up, and even if he did, their bed wasn't exactly set up for bondage. "Nah, I'm not ready to get all kinky yet."

"That's what I thought." Rhys reached down to stroke Peter's hair. "That being said, shut the fuck up and suck my cock."

Peter chuckled slightly. He reached down to take the hard member in his hand, then began to run his tongue around the soft head. It was one thing he loved about sucking cock, that something so soft could at the same time be so very hard. His tongue licked at the slit, tasting the saltiness of Rhys. He pushed in a little, wanting to get every drop of the salty goodness from his lover. He began to lick the underside of the hard shaft, going from soft tip to even more delicate balls. He used his lips to pull at the delicate skin, knowing how much Rhys liked it, before he took the delicate orbs into his mouth. His tongue ran over the balls, gently probing and lifting before he let one then the other slip from his mouth. He nudged them with his nose as he pushed Rhys's legs up giving him better access to the man's tight pink hole. He breathed deeply, smelling Rhys, a smell he would know anywhere.

"Oh God, Peter," Rhys moaned as Peter began to lick his inner hole. He reached down and began to stroke his cock, using his whole hand on his throbbing member.

Peter stabbed at the hole with his tongue, trying to gain entrance. He licked around the hole, getting the area wet before he pushed his finger in. He twisted and turned the digit around and around, his tongue pushing beside the finger.

"Fuck, Peter!"

Peter put his mouth to the tight hole and began to suck.

"Fuck!" Rhys arched his back, his fist tearing at the sheets.

Peter smiled against the smooth skin before he sucked hard on the tight puckered hole. Rhys moaned, his head thrashing from side to side. Peter pushed his tongue in as far as he could get it, thrusting it in and out. He pushed Rhys's legs up, further opening the man's ass.

"Oh God!"

Peter slid two fingers into Rhys's hole and thrust them in and out. Rhys jerked his cock hard and fast, his body covered with a fine sweat as he trembled with lust. Peter removed his fingers. He placed his mouth back over the open hole and once again tongue-fucked his lover. He alternated between sucking and tongue fucking, knowing he was driving Rhys into a state of orgasmic bliss.

"Oh! Oh! Oooohhhhh!" Rhys cried out as he came, string after string of white pearl hitting his chest.

Peter let go of Rhys's legs. He crawled up along Rhys's side and leaned down to lick the cum off his chest.

"Damn you taste good, baby." Peter smiled at him.

"Fuck" was all Rhys could say, his hand running up and down his chest.

"I take it you enjoyed that?" Peter couldn't keep the cocky grin off his face.

"Fuck!"

Peter began to laugh. He kissed Rhys's cheek before burying his face in his neck. His teeth scraped along the sensitive skin.

"I don't think I can do it again." Rhys ran his hand along Peter's back, his head tilting to the side to allow Peter better access.

"I haven't gotten off yet," Peter reminded him.

"You should have fucked me when I told you to."

Peter placed his chin on Rhys's shoulder so he could look at him. "You could give me a blow job."

Rhys closed his eyes. "I'm in a state of sexual bliss right now. Maybe when my bones stop being liquid, I'll think about it."

"Oh really?" Peter asked, his eyebrow cocked.

Rhys laughed. Pushing Peter onto his back, Rhys straddled his legs. "Hand me the lube, baby."

Peter reached up and grabbed the lube, then handed it over. Rhys poured a little on his hand, then reached down and began to stroke Peter's cock, making sure to slick his member. Placing a little more lube on his fingers, Rhys reached around and inserted them into his hole, then worked and stretched it, preparing. He raised up, lined the hard cock up with his hole, and slid down on it slowly.

"It feels so good," Peter moaned.

Rhys began to move slowly up and down, his hips rolling as he came down. He began to move faster, his cock bouncing up and down, slapping Peter's abdomen. Peter reached for Rhys's cock and stroked it a little, knowing Rhys wouldn't come again so soon, but that didn't mean he didn't want to touch his cock.

"You feel so good, so fucking tight." Peter moaned as Rhys started squeezing the muscles of his ass, grabbing Peter's cock and pulling it in. "God, I'm going to come if you keep that up."

Rhys laughed. "Then come for me, baby. You don't have to wait for me."

Peter tossed his head back, groaning as Rhys continued to use his ass muscles to grip and pull his cock. He felt the tingle low in his abdomen, his balls rising up.

"Fuck, Rhys, I'm going to come, I don't want to come already."

Rhys laughed. "Then I'm doing it right."

"Fuck, Rhys, baby," Peter panted, trying to keep from shooting. Try as he might, though, he couldn't stop, the feeling of Rhys's ass just too good. He shot hard and deep. Rhys's ass continued to grip him, milking every last drop from his still twitching cock.

"I love it when I make you come fast," Rhys murmured, lying against Peter.

Peter pulled his cock out of Rhys's ass, his arms going around his lover as Rhys snuggled against him and closed his eyes.

Chapter 13

PETER LOOKED up from his work. He could swear he heard voices. Nothing loud or close enough to make out the words but loud enough to be slightly annoying. He walked to the window and looked out expecting to see someone standing in the yard, perhaps talking to Rhys. He looked back and forth, but no one was there.

Peter walked to one of the other windows, looking for the speaker, yet nothing was there. He could hear crying now, a soft sobbing that grew in intensity. He began to walk through the house, trying to find the source of the sound. He had heard that a baby rabbit often sounded like someone crying. Had a cat trapped a rabbit somewhere?

He headed up the stairs, hearing the shower come on.

"Rhys?" he called again. The voices had stopped, yet the crying continued.

"Rhys? Are you in the shower?" he opened the bathroom door, the heat from the water steaming up the windows. The crying grew louder now.

"Rhys? Did you hurt yourself?" He reached for the shower door.

Suddenly a hand slammed against the shower door, leaving a print in the steam as it slid down. Peter jumped back and grabbed the sink behind him as his heart beat faster than he thought possible.

"Rhys!" He reached for the shower door, truly believing Rhys had fallen. He slid the door open, but the shower was empty.

"Rhys!" he yelled again, turning around and looking for the person who was just in the shower.

"What, Peter?" Rhys asked, standing in the bathroom door. "You know, you're going to use all the hot water."

"Where were you?" Peter grabbed Rhys's shoulders and ran his hands ran all over his body, assuring himself that the man wasn't hurt. He knew logically Rhys hadn't been in the shower, but the fear was there and very real.

"Widow's walk. Remember I told you I was going to take my laptop up there and work. It's a beautiful day out. Peter, you really need to get out of the house a little." He placed his hands on Peter's waist, forcing him to take a step back.

"You weren't just in the shower?"

Rhys shook his head. "No, why would I be?"

Pete looked around the room once more, his heart rate slowing. "No reason. You're right. I need to take a breather. I thought I heard you crying in the shower."

"Why would I be in the shower crying?" Rhys asked, reaching in to turn the water off.

Peter shook his head, his hands rubbing his face.

"Sweetheart, take a break. Take a walk and clear your head. The book can wait another few hours."

Peter gave a deep sigh. Glancing back at the shower, he gave a slight nod. "You're right. I need to take a break. Maybe I'll just go outside for a while, take my camera, and see what strikes my fancy."

Rhys gave him a deep kiss. "I'll be here waiting for your return. How do you feel about having a salad tonight? The weather has been simply beautiful today, and I got a few fresh vegetables from the farmers market."

"A salad will be fine." Peter ran his hands through his hair as he exhaled loudly. "I need to clear my head, maybe go away for a few days."

"If we go away for a few days, you won't have any fun. You'll spend the whole time worrying about the fact that you have a deadline to meet."

"I'm hearing things, Rhys. I hear voices. I hear sobbing. I see shadows. There is the feeling I'm being watched. I see a dark-haired man staring at me from the windows. There was a handprint in the steam. Either I'm going crazy, or the house is haunted. Please tell me I'm not having a psychotic break."

Rhys pulled him into his arms. "You're not having a psychotic break, baby. We've both heard noises—doors slamming and so forth. I will admit there is something different about the house. I'm not sure I believe in ghosts, but I will admit that not everything can be explained away."

Peter slid his arms around Rhys, letting the man hold him close and comfort him.

"You put yourself under a lot of stress. Who cares if you don't get four books out this year? Take a year off writing and just relax. It isn't like either of us really needs to work anyway."

"Like I could just sit around for a year. Hell, like I could tell my editor no when she calls and says 'can you write a story over…' well, whatever."

"Learn to say no, baby. You try to please everyone, and in the long run you hurt yourself. Take a few days and forget about writing. Sit outside and read, paint a few rooms, whatever. Take a few days to just relax, and you'll be amazed how the sounds you think you hear go away and the story ideas flow."

Peter snuggled into Rhys's arms, his face going against his neck as he breathed the scent of him. When his world became chaotic, he would just snuggle into Rhys's arms, and the smell of his skin and the sound of his breathing always brought a sense of calmness to Peter that meditating never had.

"Take a walk, Peter, let the land clear your senses. Maybe you can come up with a few ideas. When's the last time you blogged? I think you have been neglecting that. Perhaps you can get a few pictures to post on your website."

"You're right." Peter stepped away from Rhys, taking the man's hand as he did. "You go ahead and work on your game. I'll go find my camera and explore."

"I would love to spend the day in your arms, baby, but the game really is demanding my attention. Do you even know where your camera is?"

"Yeah, I have it in my office." He sighed. "I made sure I put it in there when I unpacked it."

Rhys gave him a kiss. "Exploring will relax you, baby. It'll clear the cobwebs from your mind, and you'll be able to focus on your writing more."

Peter rubbed his forehead. "Yeah. I'm going to grab my camera."

"Don't forget to take a bottle of water with you." Rhys called as Peter stepped out of the bathroom and into the hallway.

"I'll grab one," Peter promised.

"Peter, baby, I love you." Rhys blew him a kiss before he walked up the stairs to his own office.

"I love you too, sweetie."

Peter walked across his office, looking out the window as he went. He stopped for a moment. He thought he saw someone standing under the tree, so he stepped closer to the window and looked down at the ground, but nothing was there. Shaking his head, he picked up his camera and left the office. He walked down the hallway and glanced in the bathroom, but he was almost afraid of what he would see. When had he become afraid of his own house, afraid to look in his own bathroom? He hadn't been hurt. Nothing threatened him, yet he couldn't shake the feeling of fear.

Chapter 14

PETER WALKED down the small worn path that led to the cluster of trees behind the house. Cold weather was just around the corner. True, today was sunny and hot, but the leaves had already begun their change and started falling to the ground below. He stared at the branches, the rich colors of the leaves, the sunlight reflecting off them. Taking his camera, he focused on the canopy above him. He stared through the lens for a moment before he took the picture. He loved to take pictures, to capture a moment in time that would never happen again. At one time he had thought about becoming a photographer, but there really wasn't a big demand for that. So now he took his own photos and used them as inspiration for his books. Sometimes he put his pictures on his website. He had gotten several compliments for them but had never really gotten the courage to do a photography book. Perhaps one day he would submit a book of his pictures to a publishing house, if he ever got enough pictures that he felt were good enough. It was also a way to relax after book signings, book deadlines, and many other pressures that came with writing.

He continued down the path and stopped to take pictures from different angles, different settings, using a variety of colors to give each shot, although of the same tree, a different perspective.

He turned in a slow circle, listening to the trees, the way the leaves rustled. This would be the perfect spot for a cabin, a small garden in the corner, lovers hiding among the trees not worrying about anyone catching them. He continued to turn, his mind trying to lay out the scene, when he caught something out of the corner of his eye.

"Hello?" Peter called, sure he had seen someone in the undergrowth—just a glimpse of shirt maybe. "Hello, is anyone there?"

Silence was the response. It was the wind that rustled the leaves, but nothing more. He walked on, pushing branches aside, and to his left he saw something dart again.

"Hello," he tried once more. "You don't have to hide. I don't care if you're on my land."

He hurried in the direction he was sure he saw the person. Pushing through the brush, he entered a small clearing. Peter stopped and looked round. It was still, the leaves not moving, silent.

"Hello?" he called once again, feeling a bit silly this time. Obviously, whoever he saw wasn't going to make himself known. It was probably just a boy, someone who came to pick apples or blackberries and was afraid he was in trouble for trespassing.

"It was okay, really," he whispered.

The wind suddenly started to blow, and the leaves flew into the air. He felt like he was in a tornado. The trees began to bend. He closed his eyes, and raised his hands to cover his face and protect himself from the bits of twigs and leaves that pelted him.

"I'm sorry."

Peter jerked around. He had heard a voice. He was sure of it.

"Hello?" he called again. "It's okay, really it is."

The wind suddenly stopped.

Peter looked around the small clearing. "Hello? If you want to pick fruit, it's okay."

He was greeted once again by silence. He shook his head. "I have got to be losing my mind. It has to be the wind. I wanted to hear something, so I heard it. Rhys is right. I'm working way too hard."

He looked at the clearing once again. This would be a wonderful picnic spot. If he could remember exactly how to get here, he might just bring Rhys back. Peter started to take pictures of the clearing, the beginning of a story already forming. He would bring Rhys out later. He was sure Rhys would find use for the clearing also.

"Get rid of him." The voice seemed to float through the trees

113

"Get rid of who?" Peter looked around, trying to decide exactly where the voice was coming from.

"*I want you to be mine.*"

Peter looked in all directions, stepping out of the clearing and into the trees. "Alexey? Is that you, Alexey?"

The breeze ruffled his hair, and his body tingled as if someone had wrapped their arms around him. His skin ached for a solid touch that wasn't there.

"I want to help you, Alexey. Is it Demetri? He hurt you, didn't he? The bruises I saw, he did that to you didn't he?"

"*Protect me.*"

Peter wove his way through the trees. "I don't know how to help you. Is Demetri here? Is he the ghost in the house?"

The wind began to blow, leaves whipping up to form a dust devil. It wove through the trees moving closer to Peter. He stood there unable to move, his feet frozen in place. The swirling mass moved closer picking up more leaves as it went. In the middle Peter thought he saw a young man, his jeans hung low on his hips, his chest bare. He was staring at Peter, a look of determination on his face.

"*Get rid of him, Peter. Get him out of our house.*"

"Get who out? Demetri? Is he in our house? I don't know how to help you."

The figure rushed at him. Peter threw his hands up to protect himself, but the wind dissipated just before it reached him.

"Alexey? Alexey, wait. You have to tell me how to help you." Peter looked around, but Alexey was gone.

"DID YOU get many good pictures while you were exploring?" Rhys asked, nodding to the camera.

"Yeah, I got a few pretty good ones. The leaves are amazing, so many colors. I found a little clearing while I was exploring. It was almost like a little secret hideaway. We really need to get in there and clean out some of that underbrush." He leaned in to give Rhys a kiss, grabbing an olive from the can as he did. "I found a great meditation spot and even greater picnic spot. We have to go out there some afternoon, maybe have sex, eat a little, have more sex."

"It would probably be easier to hire someone to do that."

"For sex?" Peter teased him. "If you wish, but I would think that was something you wanted to do yourself."

"For the landscaping." Rhys smacked him on the ass.

Peter shook his head, a smile on his face as he blew Rhys a kiss. "We can do it. It'll take a while, but I think if we got some equipment we could start clearing and landscaping the area."

Rhys leaned back against the counter. "Where did you get your landscaping degree?"

"The same place I got my interior design degree, my handyman degree, and my lawn maintenance degree," he snarked. "You're the one who wanted all this land. You said it would be great for us."

"I didn't say I wanted to clear it myself," Rhys pointed out. "We can just hire someone for the landscaping."

"Rhys, think of it as a bonding moment."

Rhys shook his head. "I don't bond over manual labor. I hire really hot guys to do that while I stand in the window and watch."

"I'm not sure I approve of you watching really hot guys work while I slave away at a computer. I'm supposed to be the only hot guy you like to watch."

Rhys grabbed Peter's lower lip with his teeth, his forehead resting against Peter's. "I said look at, not touch. You're still the only one for me."

Peter jumped as the sound of a door slamming sounded somewhere in the house. "Ow," he muttered, touching his lip to see a faint trace of blood.

"I'm sorry." Rhys frowned. "The slamming door startled me. Did you leave a window open?"

"It's nice outside but not nice enough to leave a window open. You know how I never remember to close them, and it's too cool at night to have one open."

"Go check for me, will you? I'll finish the salad and bring it into the dining room." He kissed Peter softly on the lips. "I really am sorry I bit you."

Peter smiled. "It was an accident. Hell, I might have done the same thing if the lip was between my teeth."

"Don't be long." Rhys started tossing the salad.

Peter jogged up the steps two at a time, heading for the upper landing. He opened the first room and checked to make sure the window was closed. He pulled the door closed and moved to the next room. After checking that one, he closed the door. Peter turned suddenly when he heard the shower turn on. He headed slowly down the hall toward the bathroom. He knew Rhys was downstairs, but he wanted to tell himself Rhys was in the bathroom. His heart was beating loudly, and his hand trembled. He stood before the open bathroom door, trying to gather the courage to enter. Taking a deep breath, he closed his eyes to calm his nerves.

"Rhys, are you in the bathroom?"

Silence was his answer.

"Rhys?" he tried again, moving slowly.

"Have you checked the rooms yet, Peter?" Rhys called from the bottom of the stairs. "Dinner is on the table."

"Just a moment," Peter called. Breathing deeply to steel his nerves, he stepped into the bathroom. The hot water had made the mirror steam over. He stepped to the shower and slid the door open. It was empty, the hot water on full blast. Peter reached in and turned off the faucet as relief flooded his body.

"Just old plumbing," he muttered to himself.

"Peter!" Rhys called again.

"Coming!" he yelled, turning around "Fuck!"

"What, Peter?"

Peter stared at the mirror—the word HELP was clearly written in the steam.

"Nothing," he murmured, swiping the word from the mirror with his hand.

"What?" Rhys asked, appearing in the doorway.

Peter screamed, his hand going to his chest. "Fuck! Tell me when you're coming up behind me. I'm going to have to start putting bells on your shoes."

"You hollered, why?"

"The shower turned on again." He turned to look at the bathroom mirror. The word and steam were gone.

"What?"

Peter opened the shower. It was dry as a bone. "The shower was running. The hot water caused the mirror to steam over."

Rhys reached down and touched the bottom of the shower. "It's dry, Peter. It couldn't have been on."

"But…." Peter didn't know what to say. "I know what I saw, Rhys."

"Come down and have supper." He slid his arm around Peter's waist. "I think you're tired and your imagination is getting the best of you."

"Stress from writing too much?"

Rhys leaned against Peter, snuggling into his arms. "It is probably a loose knob or something. We can call a plumber out and have him look at it in the morning. The sound of a door slamming was probably just a branch hitting the side of the house. We can get a landscaper hired and he will trim up the trees. I bet once we get the trees trimmed back we won't hear the mysterious door slamming."

"Loose washers? Tree branches?" Peter snorted.

"Fine, the house is haunted by someone named Alexey. Let's call a paranormal research team."

Peter pulled out of Rhys's embrace. "Don't humor me. I know what I saw. This house is haunted. I'm sure of it. I think I knew it the day we moved in. Maybe you think I'm crazy, but this house is haunted."

Rhys smoothed his hair. He wrapped his arms around his lover's waist once again and hugged Peter close. "I think right after we moved in, you developed writer's block. You said yourself—the story ideas aren't there. You sit, facing the computer every day, forcing yourself to write. That's a lot of stress on anyone. Stress will make you see things that aren't there, hear things that aren't there."

Peter yanked away. "Don't patronize me, Rhys. I know what I saw. I know what I've heard. Hell, you've heard the doors slamming, seen kitchen cabinets open. It isn't the house settling. It isn't stress. This house is fucking haunted, and I'll prove it to you even if it kills me."

"Peter…." Rhys reached for him. "I don't know what I've heard. I just can't help but believe that there is an explanation for everything we have heard that doesn't involve a ghost."

Peter turned abruptly and headed down the hall. He wasn't sure how he was going to make Rhys believe him, but he would find a way.

"Don't get all pissy with me, Peter. Just because the shower isn't wet doesn't give you the right to storm off." He followed Peter out of the bathroom and down the hall.

"I just want you to see what I see, hear what I hear." Peter stopped on the stairs. "I want you to understand that I'm not going crazy. I want you to believe me."

Rhys reached for him, but Peter turned and continued down the stairs.

"Forget it, Rhys, just forget it."

"I don't want to fight, Peter. We never fight. We've had disagreements before, usually over office space, but we've never just argued."

Peter stopped at the bottom of the steps. "Because you never thought I was crazy before."

"I don't think you're crazy," Rhys argued.

"No, just overly stressed," he whispered, heading for the dining room.

"Peter, wait, let's just look at what we know about the house, all right?" Rhys called after the retreating figure.

Peter looked up when Rhys entered. He had already placed the salad in the bowl.

"How about we watch a movie tonight?" Rhys asked as he placed a bit of the salad in his own bowl.

Peter sighed, pouring dressing on his salad as he glanced back at Rhys. "Sit down and eat, baby."

"We can do some more research on the house if you want."

"Don't." Peter stabbed his salad. "Just don't, okay."

"I don't want to fight with you, Peter. I hate people being mad at me." He shoved his salad around.

"I'm not mad at you, Rhys. I'm just frustrated. I feel like I'm going crazy. I never heard voices or saw shadows until I moved here."

"I love you," Rhys whispered, his voice cracking just a little.

Peter pushed away from the table, walked over to kneel before Rhys and took Rhys's hands in his. "I love you too, Rhys, more than life itself. I don't want to fight with you. I hate fighting as much as you do. A movie night sounds really good. You may be right. Maybe I need to take a few days and put my writing aside. I can spend my time on the Internet looking up Demetri Romanov. He was a Russian art dealer, so there has to be information about him somewhere. Maybe I can find out why he never wanted the house sold."

Rhys brought Peter's fingers to his lips, then gave them a quick kiss and smiled at Peter. "You should finish eating."

"Just remember, no matter what, I'll always love you."

Rhys's smile couldn't have gotten any bigger. "I love you too, baby, more than anything."

Chapter 15

"WHICH ONE do you want to watch?" Rhys held up the two movies.

Pete shrugged indifferently, setting the bowl of popcorn on the table. "I don't care one way or the other. Whichever one you want is fine."

"I'm thinking more adventure than romantic comedy tonight." He popped the DVD in the player. He pushed Play, then hurried over to the couch, where he curled up in Peter's arms and took the bowl of popcorn in his lap.

"You know I love you right?" Peter kissed the top of Rhys's head as he grabbed a handful of popcorn.

"I love you too, baby, now hush, the movie's starting." Rhys snuggled a little closer.

Peter smiled, settling in a little more, and from the corner of his eye he saw a shadow move.

"Could you set the water beside you?" Rhys asked, handing him the glass.

"Sure." Peter took the glass and set it on the end table, and then he turned to see the dining room more clearly. It seemed unnaturally dark, almost as if someone was blocking the door. He leaned a little, trying to see the window in the room, the dining room table, or one of the vases Rhys set as a centerpiece.

"Hold still, you're going to dump me on the floor." Rhys wiggled his ass against Peter, trying to shove Peter back a little.

Peter shook his head, his attention back on the man in his arms. "Sorry. It just seemed dark in the dining room."

"It's the new curtains you bought. I closed them before I came in." Rhys dismissed the comment.

"The new curtains?"

"Uh-huh," Rhys responded absently, his attention more on the opening of the movie than on the dining room. "They have the rubber backing. You said it would keep the cold air out."

Peter looked at the room again. Perhaps Rhys was right. It wasn't as dark now as it had been. Maybe the clouds had passed over, making it look like a man was standing in the doorframe. He shook his head, sighing. Rhys was right. His imagination was getting the better of him. "Maybe we need to get some of those curtains for the bedroom. You know I've been staying awake later and later into the night writing, yet it seems like I can't sleep once the sun shines through the window."

"I've noticed you seem to enjoy sex late at night too," Rhys remarked, sliding his hand down to rub Peter through the denim of his jeans.

"I thought you wanted to watch the movie," Peter commented, taking a bit of the popcorn.

Rhys smiled wickedly as he rubbed just a little harder. "Well, I guess if you're that interested in the movie, I can stop what I'm doing."

"Is this a trick question?" Peter nipped at Rhys's neck.

"Nope, I'm just saying if you want, you can fuck my brains out right here on the floor and when you're done, we can lie in each other's arms and watch the movie."

"I'm thinking I like option number one the most," Peter whispered in his ear, giving the delicate lobe a lick when he did.

"Watching the movie?" Rhys asked, shuddering in pleasure.

"No silly, fucking your brains out. Forget the damn movie." Peter grabbed Rhys and began to tickle him.

"Don't, Peter, you know how ticklish I am." He grabbed at Peter's wrist, trying to stop the fingers from making contact with all his ticklish spots.

"Yes, I do." Peter began to laugh as Rhys broke free, rolled off the couch, and ran around to the other side of the coffee table.

Peter lunged, but Rhys was a little more nimble. He jumped out of Peter's reach and ran up the stairs with Peter following close behind.

"You can't outrun me," Peter called, taking the stairs two at a time.

Rhys laughed, running into the first room. He pushed the door shut behind him.

"Now you're trapped." Peter stood in the doorway.

"Not really, I'm still on the other side of the room." Rhys paced the floor, waiting to make his move. His chest heaved up and down as he caught his breath, and his eyes shone bright with excitement. It had been a while since they had played with each other like this, running through the house laughing.

"Yeah, but you know what, you can't get past me." Peter smiled lazily, his arms crossed over his chest. He watched Rhys pace as he tried to decide what his best option was.

Rhys chuckled, backing closer to the wall. "You can't tickle me from all the way over there."

Peter walked slowly toward Rhys, trying to anticipate which direction he would run. Rhys feinted left, then made a dash around Peter and ran back into the hallway, Peter fast on his heels. Rhys laughed, glancing over his shoulder. He was running out of places to escape to. He ran into the bedroom, Peter closer than before. He stopped beside the bed, deciding his next move, not that it mattered. Peter was directly behind him. He grabbed Rhys around the waist knocking him onto the bed. Peter began to tickle Rhys, dodging the blows that rained down on his shoulders as Rhys tried to get Peter off him. Peter laughed, grabbed Rhys's hands, and forced them above his head. Rhys bucked his hips, trying to twist his way free.

"Oh no, you don't." Peter straddled him, not that it stopped Rhys's bucking.

Rhys laughed harder, struggling to free his arms and knock Peter off his hips. Peter adjusted his grip, forcing Rhys's hands a little higher. He leaned down and licked Rhys's face, one long slow stroke from chin to hairline.

FORGOTTEN

"Eww." Rhys turned his head, trying to get away from the tongue. It didn't help, though. Peter licked the side of his face this time.

"You keep thrusting like that and I'm going to think you want to get naked."

"Getting naked is something I plan on doing at some point. Since moving here, I've been so fucking horny. Hell, forget that, I've been fucking kinky. One of these days, you're going to have to try out some of the things you read in that book."

Peter slid his hand under Rhys's shirt to feel the smooth chest. "You know one of the things I like about this house?"

"The fact we still haven't fucked in every room?" Rhys asked, leaning up so Peter could pull off his shirt.

"Well, yeah, that's a plus, but not what I was thinking." Peter gave Rhys's chest a long slow lick.

"So tell me, oh wise one, what were you thinking?" Rhys asked, running his hands through Peter's hair.

"I was thinking, I love the fact you can't get enough sex. I must admit, I'm not sure about the newfound kinky side to you, but that is something I'll live with."

Rhys giggled, and Peter nipped at the skin along his side. Peter skimmed his nails over Rhys, who shuddered each time Peter hit a ticklish spot. He bucked against Peter again.

"Nice try." Peter grinned, his fingers seeking out a ticklish spot again.

"Peter!" Rhys laughed harder, his hips bucking and his body twisting as he grabbed for Peter's hands. "Stop!"

Peter grabbed his hands, forcing them to Rhys's side, and he leaned down and licked the side of Rhys's face. Rhys turned his head to the side, trying to wipe the wet slobber, but Peter licked that side too

"Eww, cooties again!" Rhys turned his head to wipe off the other cheek.

Peter chuckled as he adjusted his weight on Rhys's body, not wanting to be too heavy for him. He knew he outweighed Rhys by a good thirty pounds. Peter reached for Rhys's hands, wanting that connection.

"God, baby, I love you so damn much." He intertwined his fingers with Rhys's as he stared into Rhys's eyes, trying to convey all the love he felt for his spouse in a look.

"I love you more," Rhys responded, staring back.

"Forget sex, I just want to be in your arms. I want to feel you against me. I can't even begin to tell you how good it feels just to have your body touching mine, to be able to wrap my arms around you. You are like the center of the hurricane, the calm to the storm of my life." Peter rolled off Rhys. He lay on his back and looked at the ceiling. He needed to do something about that ceiling. Who put wallpaper on the ceiling anyway?

"You want to just snuggle?" Rhys asked astounded. He rolled onto his side, and propped up on his elbow.

Peter reached for Rhys and pulled him onto his chest. "Yeah, I do."

Rhys snuggled closer, getting comfortable against Peter.

"I love you too, Peter. I'll be glad every day of my life you came into the coffee shop. You were so cute in a geeky klutzy way."

Peter turned his head sideways and looked at the bedroom door. For a brief moment, he thought he saw a man standing there, staring at them, his dark eyes shining with hatred. Peter jerked, surprised that someone was in their house. He could almost feel the hatred radiating from the small dark-haired stranger. What disturbed him most was the man seemed to be staring directly at Rhys. The voice he heard in the clearing came back to him.

"Rhys, baby." Peter tried to move.

"Yes, love?" Rhys snuggled closer, his grip tightening on Peter.

Peter looked back at the door, but whatever or whoever he thought he saw was gone. "Promise me you'll be careful around here."

"What do you mean?"

Peter shook his head. "Nothing, really. I just don't want you wondering off around the farm without me knowing which direction you're going. I saw a lot of overgrown areas where snakes might hide or who knows what animal. I'd hate for you to get hurt and me not know where to look for you."

"I promise."

Peter kissed the top of his forehead. "Thank you, sweetie."

PETER WALKED through the house. Upstairs he heard a door shut.

"Rhys?" he asked, making his way up the stairs. He was dreaming. Somewhere in his mind he knew he was dreaming. They didn't have carpet on the stairs and the walls were a nice tan, not golden. Doors slammed and heavy footsteps echoed from somewhere below him, followed by the hurried footsteps of someone running down the hallway. He looked but saw nothing.

Peter continued up the steps, looking down the hallway. He walked slowly, wishing he had a weapon. In a dream you always found what you needed when you needed it. This didn't feel like a dream, though. It felt real, like he was somehow actually in the house. He could feel the polished wood of the railing. He could hear someone rummaging in the bedroom. He pushed open the bedroom door just as the bathroom door down the hall slammed shut.

"Rhys?" he asked again, his voice barely above a whisper. He turned around and stepped back into the hallway. The door to the bathroom closed, but he heard the sound of the shower door opening and closing, muffled through the thick wood door.

He walked to the bathroom, not sure why his heart was beating so rapidly. Rhys was in the shower. They had been together for eight years, knew everything there was to know about each other's body. They had showered together, yet now he trembled as he pushed open the door.

The room was hot, the steam from the shower fogging up the mirror. He could see someone moving behind the glass door.

"Rhys?" he whispered, reaching for the handle. Taking a deep breath, he opened the shower door.

The man turned suddenly, his hands coming up to protect himself.

"Who are you?" Peter demanded, shocked to see a dark-haired stranger in the shower. The man wasn't really a stranger, though. It was Alexey. He knew his name now just like he knew it the other day. The man was small-boned and delicate, his features fine and almost feminine. His wet hair hung in loose curls around his face, almost to his shoulders.

The man stared at him, his hands dropping now that he no longer felt he needed to defend himself. "You left me. You said you would protect me and love me."

"Alexey?" Peter whispered. "You were just a dream."

"A dream? Was I a dream in the clearing, Peter? Was I a dream when you made love to me?"

Peter shook his head, unsure what to believe at the moment. "I asked the librarian about you. She said you never existed."

Alexey glanced over his shoulder at the open bathroom door. "Because some old woman only remembers that bastard, I never existed. Could you close the door?"

Peter ran his hands through his hair, a slight headache forming in the base of his skull. He reached out and shut the door. "I want to help you, Alexey, but I have no idea where to start. I looked through newspapers. I looked all over the Internet. All I can find is Demetri Romanov was a confirmed bachelor and a very well-respected art dealer."

Alexey snorted and turned his attention back to Peter. "Yes, no one would ever question such an educated and well-respected man. My parents sure in the hell didn't when they sent me off with him."

Peter stared at him before what the man said dawned on him. "The story I started to write, the one where the parents told their son to go to America and avoid the war. That was about you, wasn't it? How can I have been such an idiot? I didn't even put two and two together, yet I used your names."

"I wanted you to know. I wanted you to listen."

"I still don't know how to help."

"Tell me you would love me. Tell me I'm as special to you as Rhys is. Tell me you would have never let that bastard touch me. Would you stay with me, Peter?"

Peter nodded. "I would have never let anyone hurt you."

"Rhys hurts me, Peter. Make him go away."

"How can he hurt you?"

"By loving you so completely. Get rid of him. Don't leave things to me."

"Wait a minute." Peter took a step closer to the shower. He reached out to grab Alexey's wrist. He could actually feel the wet skin in his hand.

"He's coming. Hide, he's coming," Alexey whimpered, the hot water from the shower giving his skin a nice pink glow.

"Who's coming? Who do you need to be protected from? Is it Demetri? Is he here too?"

"Would you have loved me? Would you have protected me?" Alexey was frantic now, his eyes wide with fear. He reached for Peter, and his hand left a wet imprint on Peter's shirt. "Would you keep me safe, even if Rhys doesn't believe?"

"Tell me how to help you," Peter pleaded. He could actually feel the hand, the dampness soaking through his shirt. You didn't feel things in a dream, did you?

The bathroom door flew open. Alexey tore his eyes from Peter to the man who had just entered.

"Can't you do anything right, slut!" the man roared.

"Please, Demetri," Alexey cried as the man knocked him to the floor. His hand flew up and hit the glass, the handprint appearing on the steam of the door.

"Fucking slut!" Demetri roared, then grabbed Alexey and pulled him naked and dripping from the shower. "Get downstairs."

"I'm not dressed," Alexey cried, trying to shield himself from the blows, to cover his nudity.

"Then you should have gotten around a little faster. Our guest is here."

"Leave him alone." Peter lunged forward, reaching for Demetri. "Don't you fucking touch him!"

"Help me, Peter. Tell me you would have loved me and protected me," Alexey cried as the man yanked him off the floor by his hair and forced him down the stairs.

"Always!" Peter yelled, heading out the door, determined to stop Demetri from hurting Alexey.

"Wake up, Peter." Rhys shook him.

Peter came flying up out of the bed, knocking Rhys out of the way.

"Peter, it was a dream." Rhys reached for him, sliding his hand down Peter's back and trying to offer comfort.

Peter looked over his shoulder to see Rhys, the back of his hand touching his lip.

"Oh baby, did I hit you? I'm so sorry." He took Rhys's face in his hand and kissed the injured lip.

"You must have been having one hell of a dream." Rhys smiled. "You were tossing and turning. I think you might have kicked me a time or two. Do you want to tell me about it?"

Peter sighed deeply, rubbing the last of the sleep from his face. "I was in this house, but it wasn't ours, you know. There was a carpet on the stairs, and the walls were painted gold. The bedroom, this bedroom, was done in browns."

"If you're going to dream about the house at least give it a bit of style. I'd never do gold or brown," Rhys teased.

"I heard the shower come on. I wanted it to be you in the shower, but my heart was beating so fast because I knew that when I opened the door, it wouldn't be you."

"Who would it be, baby?" Rhys rubbed his shoulders.

He shook his head. "Alexey. He seemed so shocked I was there. He was standing under hot water, and the room was full of steam. I could feel the steam. I could feel his fear. My heart was beating so fast. Then this man, Demetri, burst in the door. He knocked him down, telling him he should have already been out and dressed, but I had the feeling that he wasn't really given the time, you know. Like the man had sex with him, told him to get in the shower and get downstairs, but he couldn't have been in the shower more than five minutes before he grabbed him and yanked him out. Alexey was telling Demetri he needed clothes, but Demetri said that their guest was there and if he wanted clothes, he should have been dressed already. He was forcing him to go downstairs nude, and the fear that was in his eyes as he looked back at me…."

"It was just a dream, baby." Rhys placed a gentle kiss on his shoulder. "It was probably because you and I had discussed your latest story idea before bed."

"But to have our house in my dream, to feel the fear."

"It's only natural you put our house in the dream, but you admitted that the house was ugly."

Peter chuckled, some of the tension leaving his body as Rhys started to kiss his back.

"But to have such an evil man," he protested.

"You were discussing one of your paranormal stories with me before bed. You know the editor wanted it to be heavy on the domination. You and I were talking about adding some S and M to our relationship in order for you to write it more accurately. It was your subconscious, nothing more. Don't worry much about it."

Peter breathed deeply, hoping to clear his head. "I know you're right. Everything just seemed so real."

Rhys pulled him into his arms as he lay back down. "Snuggle up to me, baby. Everything will be all right."

Peter lay back in Rhys's arms, his head on the man's chest, listening to the beating heart. He stared into the darkness, trying to shake the lingering fear. In the corner for just the briefest moment, he could have sworn he saw Alexey. Peter lifted his head to get a better look, but nothing was there.

"Go to sleep, baby. I'll protect you."

Peter smiled. "Isn't it me who should protect you?"

"Hmmm," Rhys murmured sleepily. "Now I get that chance."

Peter snuggled closer. It was nice to be held. He closed his eyes and let sleep take him.

Chapter 16

"HEY, BABY, your office looks really good." Peter stood in the attic door.

Rhys wiped the sweat from his forehead with the back of his hand. "I love the room I have up here. I have more than enough space for the storyboards. I have the posters of my games over here and on the far wall I have the cardboard cutouts."

Peter looked around the room.

"Do you want to know something really cool?" Rhys grabbed his hand and pulled him further into the room. "I have room for more than one storyboard. I have two more games I'm plotting out already. I couldn't do that when we lived in the city."

"This is a really cool room." Peter stood looking at the second and third storyboards.

"I feel so much better now that my office is done."

"I felt the same way about mine. It was great to be able to hang the posters of my book covers. We never had the room to display our stuff back in the city."

Rhys sashayed over to him. "One more reason why buying this house was such a great idea."

Peter slid his arms around Rhys's waist as Rhys leaned in and rested his forehead against Peter's. It was one of Peter's favorite things, to feel the breath of his lover skimming across his skin, to feel the heat from his body and the reassurance that he was loved.

"I should let you get back to work," Peter whispered.

"There's no hurry." Rhys began to sway back and forth, dancing to unheard music.

Peter kissed him, his body also swaying, matching Rhys's rhythm. His tongue slipped past Rhys's lips and into his warm mouth. His arms went around Rhys's waist and pulled him closer. They continued to dance around the attic, content to be with each other.

"You know what, baby? It's such a beautiful day I think I'm going to take a walk."

Rhys stepped away from him. "Where are you going? I don't want you to get hurt and I don't know where to look."

Peter smiled as Rhys parroted his words back to him. "I'm going to head south. There is this little trail that leads through the apple trees. In the middle of all those trees, there is this clearing, which I love because for a little bit I can forget that people exist. I get all kinds of story ideas there."

"Okay, sweetie." Rhys kissed his nose. "I'll be up here for a while more. I am determined to finish this game so I can spend time with you exploring the land we bought."

"Don't overdo it."

"You be careful."

PETER WALKED along the narrow trail that led to the clearing he had found. He needed to be out of the house today. The bright sunlight and the warm air with just the faintest traces of fall called to him.

He looked around the clearing, happy that he had a place he could come to and relax. It was a place where he could forget the world around him, forget modern society existed. He spread the blanket under the tree, then turned in a slow circle, enjoying the silence.

"*Peter.*" It seemed as if the trees called softly to him.

He shook his head, the sound no more than a murmur on the wind. He took a deep breath, tilted his head back, and let the wind caress his face. He needed to meditate, to clear his head of all thoughts before he went back in to finish the book.

"*Love me, Peter*" came the voice again.

"Alexey?" Peter looked around but saw nothing. He sat in front of the nearest tree, his back against the rough bark. Closing his eyes, he tried to clear his mind. He needed to work through a couple of areas in his story, and sometimes the only way he could do that was to stop thinking about his story.

It wasn't long before he felt the tension leave his body as he drifted off to sleep.

"You're home early." Alexey smiled at Peter as he entered the house.

"Who are you?"

Alexey's smile faltered just a little. "I know it's a different color than normal, but no need to pretend you don't know me. Do you like me with blond hair? I can go back to brown if you don't."

"Where's Rhys?" Peter looked around the house.

"Rhys who, baby? I think you're working way too hard. Didn't you name one of your characters Rhys?"

"I'm married to Rhys."

Alexey tilted his head to one side, a worried expression on his face. "You married me, baby, three years ago, remember?"

Peter sat on the couch. "Alexey?"

"You remember, don't you? What happened? Did you hit your head?" Alexey sat on the couch, drawing his legs under him.

Peter reached over to take Alexey's hand. "Working way too hard, you're right. Can I have a kiss?"

Alexey's smile could have lit a stadium. "Always. You know I love to kiss you."

"Did you leave Demetri?"

A shadow passed over Alexey's face. "Demetri who? It's been just you and me, Peter. I think you need a nice back rub. You need to relax, and you always said I had magic fingers.

"You do have magic fingers." Peter took the man's hands. He kissed each finger before moving to kiss the palm of each hand and

finally the inner wrist. Peter stared at the wrist for a moment. Faint red marks marred the otherwise flawless skin. "What happened?"

"It's nothing." Alexey pulled his hands from Peter's.

"It doesn't look like nothing. Are those rope burns?"

Alexey laughed, but it seemed a little forced. "Rope burns? Come on, Peter, when have you ever tied me up?"

Peter shook his head. "You're right. I don't know what I was thinking."

"You have always been a kind and considerate lover."

Peter kissed him again. "Thank you."

"I've been thinking," Alexey began, his voice a bit hesitant.

"What about?"

"Well...." Alexey looked around for a moment before meeting Peter's eyes. "I want us to get married again. The first time it was such a small ceremony, we couldn't afford much. Now that you are a successful writer I want a large wedding. Marry me again, Peter."

"Alexey we can't get married. I'm married to Rhys, and you're... well...." He didn't know how to finish the sentence.

"I'm what, Peter?" Alexey sat back, his arms across his chest.

"You're in a relationship with Demetri."

Alexey rolled his eyes as he shook his head. "There is no one named Demetri, Peter. There is just you and me. I think I need to call the doctor and have him look at you."

"I probably do need a good shrink," Peter muttered. "Tell me, Alexey, is Demetri haunting the house?"

"Demetri? Of course not, Peter."

RHYS WALKED along the small path, swinging the picnic basket and whistling a simple tune. He wished he was good at whistling, but he was more of a monotone type. He stopped suddenly. Someone was sitting by Peter, touching his hair.

"Hey! Who are you?" Rhys called out. It was obvious Peter was asleep.

133

The man jerked his head up. Rhys pushed aside the branch of a bush as the man disappeared. He stopped in the clearing, looking around. There was no way someone could just disappear.

"Hey!" he yelled again.

"Rhys?" Peter sat up, rubbing his eyes. "I must have fallen asleep. I'm sorry."

"I thought I saw someone," Rhys muttered.

"Who?"

He shook his head, setting the picnic basket down. "I don't know. I blinked and he was gone."

"Maybe it was just a trick of the light," Peter offered.

Rhys spread the blanket on the ground.

"I think the picnic is a romantic idea." Peter grabbed Rhys's hips and pulled him for a kiss.

"It's just a salad, nothing exciting really, but I thought I'd surprise you."

"Are you going to be my dessert?" Peter asked, licking Rhys's chin. "If you are, can we go straight to dessert?"

"It's a little cool to be thinking about sex."

"It'll be the perfect way to warm up."

"I should be flattered after this many years you still want to fuck like a little rabbit." Rhys sat on the blanket and began to pull out the bowls.

"I can't help it, so sue me if I find my husband to be more attractive and desirable as the years go by." Peter sat beside Rhys.

"I'm glad you do. So did you have a nice nap?"

Peter opened the salad dressing and began to pour it on his salad. "It was odd. I dreamed I came home, but it was to someone named Alexey. He was asking me how I liked his new hair color. I asked where you were, but he said he was married to me and you were nothing more than a part of some book I was writing."

"You don't normally have such odd dreams," Rhys commented, taking the dressing from him.

"I don't normally dream about the same person over and over, but since moving here I am. Maybe these dreams are a way our ghost is asking for help."

"You still think the house is haunted?"

Peter nodded. "I do, and the more time I spend here, the more I believe it's haunted. You can't tell me that you aren't thinking the same thing."

Rhys sighed softly. "I'll admit there have been some things happening I can't explain. I'm not sure I want to admit the house is haunted, though. I was raised to believe that ghosts don't exist. There is always a logical explanation for everything if you look for it.'

"Humor me, Rhys."

Rhys nodded. "Maybe do some of our own ghost hunting. Do a little EVP work or something. I mean, if the library hasn't given us results and you have found nothing about Alexey on the Internet, maybe we can get an idea of where to start looking. Maybe Alexey will tell us his last name or something."

Peter leaned over and kissed him. "Thank you for doing this with me, babe."

"Hey, I said for better or worse. We have to stick together and work through this. It's you and me, baby, and no ghost is going to drive us apart."

RHYS BEGAN to wipe down the kitchen counters. He hated nothing more than a dirty or cluttered kitchen. He hummed a little tune as he carried the damp cloth into the washroom and dropped it into the washing machine. Now that his kitchen was in order, he could start fixing them something to eat. Maybe he would make Peter a cake for dessert. Peter would like that. Rhys really wasn't a cake person, so it was rare that Peter got one. Peter had been under a lot of stress, though, and making a cake would be a nice way to let Peter know how much Rhys loved him. He sighed. He knew Peter believed the house was haunted, and the truth was Rhys had a nagging suspicion Peter might be right, not that Rhys was ready to admit it yet. Too many things happened that he couldn't explain—slamming doors, the water turning on and off. He would set something on the counter only to find it gone, but above all, he often felt a sense of hatred, like something didn't want him here. He felt it most when he was alone, but turning on the radio often got rid of the feeling. He was sure it was just the fact he had never lived in the country before. Hell, other than a duplex, he never had a house before, and he really didn't call a duplex a house.

He walked around the kitchen, getting the ingredients he needed. It drove him crazy to watch Peter cook. The man would read the recipe, then walk around and get the items as he needed them. Rhys liked to have everything sitting in front of him within easy reach.

He walked over to turn on the radio. Maybe he couldn't carry a tune in a bucket, but that didn't stop him from singing along with the radio as he cooked or cleaned.

"*Mine*" came the whisper.

Rhys continued to sing off-key with the song on the radio. He set everything on the counter, then turned and leaned down to get a mixing bowl from one of the lower cabinet doors. The door above him swung fully open on silent hinges. As Rhys stood, his forehead slammed into the corner of the door. The pain ripped through his body, and he reached up to touch the spot on his forehead. His vision began to blur, his body became light, and for the first time in his life, he thought he was going to faint.

"HEY, BABE, what do you need?" Peter asked.

Rhys stood in the kitchen doorway. He stared unblinking at Peter, his body swaying slightly, his arms wrapped around his waist. He was hunched in on himself, as if the only place he could find comfort was in his own arms.

"Rhys, what happened?" Peter pushed back the chair and noticed the small trickle of blood on Rhys's forehead.

"I hit my head," Rhys murmured softly.

"Oh baby." Peter reached up and wiped away the thin line of blood. "Are you okay? Do you need to go to the doctor?"

Rhys shook his head, looking at the ground. He seemed to hug himself a little tighter. "Kiss?"

"Of course, baby." Peter kissed him gently on the lips before reaching up to kiss the small cut on his forehead. "To make it all better."

Rhys blinked once, then twice. His forehead wrinkled in confusion as he looked at Peter. "Make what all better?"

"The cut on your head."

Rhys reached up to touch his forehead. "How the hell?"

"You said you hit your head." A look of concern crossed Peter's face as he looked Rhys in the eyes. "Maybe I need to take you to the doctor. You might have a concussion or something."

"I'm fine. I've been working on that new video game, and I think I'm getting spacey. I decided to take a break from the game and do a little cooking. You know how cooking relaxes me, clears my head. I was singing to the radio, getting the stuff ready to make you a cake. I turned to grab a mixing bowl, and that's about it. I don't remember hitting my head. I only vaguely remember walking in here."

Peter kissed the tip of Rhys's nose. "You always zone out when you're working on a game, almost as bad as I do when I'm writing. Your mind was probably more on the game than what you were doing, which is why you don't remember hitting your head. You can cook in your sleep, and it would turn out fantastic. Hell, half the time I think you're on autopilot when you're in the kitchen."

"Yes, I do tend to zone out when writing up a code for a game, but never this bad." He gave a soft sigh as he shook his head. "Never this bad, you think I'd remember hitting my head hard enough to have a goose egg and blood."

Peter hugged Rhys close for a moment before stepping away. "Maybe we should go away for a couple of days, forget about deadlines."

Rhys shook his head. "We can't forget deadlines. Maybe afterward? I think the beach would be nice."

Peter hugged him tight. "Promise you that."

Rhys shook his head. "I'll start supper. What do you want to eat?"

Peter looked at his computer. He wasn't in the mood to write anymore. "Why don't we go to town and get something?"

"There aren't a lot of choices in town. Besides, I was going to make you a cake. I have everything out." Rhys touched his forehead again. "Do you think I'm going to have a goose egg or an ugly bruise?"

Peter kissed his forehead once again. "Of course not. I just kissed it better. Have you started putting the things in the bowl, or is everything on the counter? You can always leave it there and make me a cake when we come home. How about Mexican food tonight?"

"You want me to just leave things?" Rhys was taken aback. He knew he was a bit anal at times, but he couldn't just walk out the door with things sitting on the counter.

Peter chuckled. "Live life on the edge, Rhys."

"You do want me to enjoy dinner?" Rhys asked, his eyebrow cocked.

Peter kissed the tip of his nose. "I'll make sure anything perishable is put up, and you get ready."

"Let me change my shirt and put some ice on my forehead, and I'll be ready." Rhys looked a bit skeptical.

"Rhys?"

Rhys stopped in the doorway.

"I still think the house is haunted, even if you don't believe me."

Rhys gave a sigh. "It's not that I don't believe you, Peter. It's just…."

"It's just you don't believe in ghosts."

Rhys shook his head softly. "I don't know what to believe anymore."

Chapter 17

"THAT WAS really good." Rhys sighed, rubbing his full stomach as he leaned his head back against the headrest of the car seat.

"I have to admit, it was really good. You wouldn't think you could find such wonderful food out here in the sticks," Peter agreed as he started the car. "Do you want to stop and see if there's a movie we can rent or something?"

"Nah, that's okay. I need to get back to the video game. You had me leave things on the counter in the kitchen, which I have to say has really been bothering me, and you have to finish the edits for *Sticky Situations*. We both know the movie would just sit there."

"Yeah, it would." Peter stopped at the only light in town. "How come it seems no matter when I drive through town, the light is always red? I have yet to come to town and be able to just drive straight through. I think it knows I'm coming."

Rhys laughed. "There is a little gremlin who watches for your car. When you get close, it switches the light from green to red."

The light turned green, and Peter pulled forward. "Well, yeah, did you see any other cars? It's a gremlin all right. Hey, maybe that could be the basis for my next book."

"A gremlin that changes street lights whenever you approach? I don't think it would be a best seller."

"I bet people would relate to it." He turned off the main road and started down the paved country road that led to their house.

"Still not the basis for a story."

"Okay, here's one. There are a couple of big city boys who move to a small town. What they don't know is the town doesn't like outsiders moving in. The tourists are fine, which is why there's a bed and breakfast in town. Those who move in though…."

"Oh, Peter, you really are stretching with this one."

"Just hold on." He switched to his bright lights. "The town is known for its awesome barbecue. What no one knows is the smiling faces are really hiding demons. The gremlins make the newest members of the town stop at the light, and the demons grab them and drag them from the car. The unsuspecting people are taken to the butcher where they are killed and served up as barbecue."

Rhys groaned, rubbing his forehead. He shook his head in disbelief. "Where do I even start with that one?"

"What?" Peter began to slow down; his turn was coming up before long.

"Well, won't people notice that everyone who comes to town goes missing?"

"The only people who go missing are the ones that move in," Peter pointed out.

"Who are all orphans with no friends or family? After the third set of people disappear, I think outside authorities will notice a pattern."

"Well…." Peter turned onto the winding driveway that led to their home. "I'd figure something out. Maybe since they are demons, they have a mind control device that makes other people forget they existed."

"So it controls the whole world?"

"No, only the people who come to town looking for their loved ones."

Rhys shook his head, chuckling. "Oh, Peter, give it up. You can't save that wildass idea."

Peter shrugged as he shut off the car. "I may be able to save that one yet."

Rhys climbed out of the car. He shut the door and leaned against the top of the car, waiting for Peter to shut his door. "I love your conviction. I love the fact you're creative and have a mind that seems to be a never-ending source of outlandish, fun, and crazy ideas. I love that you support me in my creative endeavors. I am telling you all that to tell you that this story was dead before it even started. It's great that you tried to carry it through, but really, Peter? Demons who sell humans as the Midwest's best BBQ and gremlins that fix the stoplights so they can have the victims to do it?"

Peter flipped the keys until he held the house key. "I'll admit, it was a stretch, but it doesn't mean that a really awesome story won't come from it."

Rhys walked around the car. "I'm sure you will get an awesome story from it. That just wasn't one of your better ideas."

Peter started up the steps. "I'm still not going to admit that the story is a failure."

Rhys grabbed Peter's arm and turned Peter to face him. He leaned in and gave Peter a kiss. "You wouldn't be the man I loved if you did."

"You have to be the best kisser in all of America." Peter returned the kiss, pushing the door in behind him. He continued backward, knowing the table was behind him somewhere.

"Let me shut the door." Rhys broke the kiss. "What the fuck?"

Peter turned around to see what had Rhys's attention. The kitchen was covered in flour and sugar.

"What the fuck happened to my kitchen?" Rhys walked around Peter, careful where he stepped. The bowls were broken and on the floor, the cabinet doors hung open, the boxes tossed around the room. "It looks like a fucking tornado hit it. We need to call the police, Peter. Someone broke into our house."

Peter walked past him, heading for the next room. "Let's make sure nothing else has been destroyed."

"My video game," Rhys gasped, rushing past him toward the staircase. "If anything's happened to that game or anything in my office for that matter, I'm so fucking killing someone."

"Rhys, wait." Peter grabbed for Rhys as he rushed past.

"What, Peter?"

He pointed to the floor. There, in the flour and sugar was one word: MINE.

"Mine what?" Rhys asked.

Peter shook his head. "I really don't know."

"We need to call the police, Peter. Someone broke into our house and destroyed our kitchen." Rhys reached into his back pocket and pulled out his cell phone. He dialed the police station.

Peter pushed open the door to the dining room and checked to see if anything else had been disturbed. The dining room seemed fine, same with the front room.

"*Peter*," a voice called from upstairs. "*Peter? Please?*"

Peter glanced over his shoulder. "Rhys?"

"*Please, Peter, you promised.*" The voice came again from somewhere upstairs.

Peter walked slowly toward the stairs. He knew Rhys was in the kitchen. "Alexey?"

"*Why, Peter?*" The voice was louder now, more of a sob.

Peter started up the stairs, the pain in the voice outweighing any fear he might have had. Maybe Rhys didn't believe the house was haunted, but he did. It was haunted by a young man named Alexey, who wanted their help.

"The police department said they would send someone out." Rhys walked out of the kitchen. "Have you noticed anything else that has been disturbed?"

Peter stopped halfway up the stairs. He debated walking the rest of the way up and trying to find Alexey.

"Peter?"

Peter glanced at the top of the stairs once more before turning around and heading back down the stairs. "From what I can tell, it was just the kitchen. Don't worry too much about it."

"Don't worry too much?" Rhys asked. "Someone broke into our house and made a mess in our kitchen."

Peter reached up to wipe a tear that had fallen. "I just don't think it was someone trying to hurt us. Halloween is next week. I'm sure it was just some kids who wanted to scare the new guys in town."

Rhys sighed. "I better wash my face. I don't want the police to think I've been crying when they get here."

Peter pulled him close one more time. "I love you so much, Rhys baby, I'll always keep you safe, I promise."

Chapter 18

"HEY, SWEETIE, are you busy?" Peter stood in the doorway to Rhys's office.

"A little bit, why?" Rhys stood at the large whiteboard, colored markers in his hand. He had several figures sketched out already, along with a few characteristics noted beside each one.

"What are you working on?" Peter walked the rest of the way into the room to lean against the desk. He didn't want to get too close to Rhys when he was drawing. Rhys always made broad gestures and turned abruptly, often either hitting or tripping over anyone who was close to him.

"Something new. I'm thinking of doing a game based on gladiators. I haven't fully decided yet, but that is popular at the moment, so I might as well cash in on the craze." Rhys stepped away from the first board and moved to the second. "This one is game three of the series, and the third board I'm think of doing something completely different than the shoot them, slash them blood-filled games I normally do. I'm thinking of something that is more mentally challenging."

Peter walked up behind him and rubbed his shoulders. "You always come up with great ideas."

Rhys took his hand and pulled it around as he kissed Rhys's fingers. "How are your books coming along?"

"I have one finished and ready to be sent to my editor."

"That's great, baby."

"After that, I have stories started, but nothing is really coming together like I want. Maybe it's because I'm not sleeping as well as I should. We got a call from the police department."

"Any news on who broke into our house?" Rhys turned around to look at Peter.

He shook his head. "Nope. They think it might have just been a random thing, probably a Halloween prank like I said. Nothing else like this has happened in town, so they think it might have been some kids from the college a few towns over. Maybe some type of initiation and our house just happened to be the first one they came to where they didn't have to worry about getting caught."

"Well, that makes me feel so much safer," Rhys said sarcastically. "Make sure we lock the doors from now on."

"We're city boys, Rhys. When do we not lock the doors?" Peter teased him.

Rhys turned back to his storyboards, reached for the black marker, and began to draw again.

"It's going to be okay, Rhys. I promise that I'll never let anyone hurt you. I promised to keep you safe, to love you forever, and always stand by your side. I meant it the day we committed to each other, and I mean it now."

Rhys smiled. "You say the sweetest things. Am I going to find those romantic words in your next book?"

Peter laughed. "You know me too well."

Rhys leaned back into Peter's arms. "I just hope the break-in doesn't keep you from sleeping. You've slept like crap since we moved in here, waking up every few hours due to nightmares, tossing and turning when you do manage to sleep. I know it takes a while to turn an empty house into a home, and every time we moved you had problems sleeping. We may have put our furniture in it, but we really haven't been here long enough to imprint our emotions and feelings into it."

"I know you're right." Peter sighed, picking up the photo on Rhys's desk. It was on the day they had committed, both of them young and ready to take on the world. The picture brought a smile to Peter's face.

Rhys began to nuzzle his neck, nipping along his shoulder. "Trust me, I'm right."

"That feels so good." Peter moaned.

"Fuck me and you'll feel better," Rhys whispered, sliding his hand down his lover's chest to the hem of his shirt. His fingers slid under the material to the smooth stomach underneath.

Peter chuckled. "Usually that is my line."

"Can I help it if I have a sudden desire for my spouse?" Rhys asked, biting Peter's shoulder a little harder.

"I think the house has started to possess you, Rhys. You rarely come on to me in such a way." Peter turned to face Rhys.

"So you should probably take advantage of it. It does happen once in a blue moon, and those are rare," Rhys teased, and he leaned in to lick Peter's neck and run his tongue along Peter's Adam's apple to the hollow underneath.

"Well, I have to admit we haven't broken your office in yet." Peter tilted his head back to allow Rhys to have better access. His body tingled, his nipple became hard nubs, and his cock stirred.

"Forget the office. I want you to fuck me on the roof." Rhys bit his chin, his teeth scraping along the firm line.

"The roof?" Peter stepped back. Rhys had never been so forceful, never so overtly sexual. "What the fuck do you mean the roof?"

"I mean the widow's walk, Peter. It's large enough and there is just something so dirty about fucking up there. I want to be taken in the sky. No one can see us, and in a way we are christening the house in a way no one else can."

Peter looked at the set of steps that led up to the widow's walk. "Sure baby. I can honestly say that's one place I've never had sex before, the roof of the house."

Rhys grabbed his hand and pulled him up the stairs. "You probably never thought about doing it on a roof before because we've never had a widow's walk before."

"I can honestly say you're right about that." He let Rhys pull him onto the roof. He looked around. It was easy to see why Rhys loved to come up here when he was working on the game. It was beautiful, and he could see forever from here. Okay, maybe not forever, but he could see a large part of the land.

"Come here." Rhys swung him around. He grabbed Peter and crushed his mouth to Peter's, his tongue forcing its way in, declaring dominance.

"You are becoming a horny little thing." Peter chuckled as Rhys grabbed his shirt and began to pull it over his head.

"I can't help it. Something about you lately drives me insane with lust every time I see you," he managed to get out between kisses.

Peter reached for Rhys's pants, and he deftly unbuttoned the fly. He really loved button-fly jeans. He yanked the fly open and moved his hands into the waistband and around Rhys's waist. He slid his hands down to cup Rhys's ass, squeezed the round globes, and pulled Rhys a little closer.

"Damn, I want you," Rhys mumbled as he continued to thrust his tongue into Peter's mouth. He sucked on Peter's tongue, tasting him.

Peter pushed Rhys's jeans down his hips. He needed Rhys closer. He wasn't sure what it was, but at the moment he didn't feel as if he could get Rhys close enough. He felt Rhys's hands in his own jeans shoving them down, the cool air caressing the newly exposed skin.

"I want you, Peter," Rhys whispered, his teeth nipping Peter's lower lip.

Peter dropped to his knees, pulling Rhys's jeans and underwear down to his knees as he did. Rhys's hard cock bounced, no longer confined by the tight jeans. Peter smiled up at Rhys, and ran his tongue along the underside of Rhys's cock from base to tip. He swirled his tongue around the tip and licked as he would an ice cream cone. His tongue pushed at the slit, tasting the saltiness. He never really enjoyed giving blow jobs before Rhys. He had hated the taste of sperm, but with Rhys it all became different. He couldn't get enough of Rhys. It was one of the ways he knew he found his other half.

He ran his hands along the back of Rhys's thighs as he took the hard cock into his mouth and down his throat. He felt Rhys's hands in his hair, pulling him closer, thrusting his cock down his throat. This was new for Rhys—he had always been the more passive partner before. Peter pulled away from the hard cock and chose instead to lick Rhys's low-hanging balls. He lifted one heavy nut with his tongue before he sucked it into his mouth. Rolling it around, he savored the taste of his lover before he took the second nut into his mouth. He loved the fact that he could take both balls into his mouth, run his tongue over them, and let them slowly slip out one by one. It was one of the few moves he had that really made Rhys's eyes roll back in his head.

"Fuck, that's good," Rhys gasped, his knees feeling week.

"Turn around and grab the railing," Peter commanded, standing to his feet.

"I have lube in my desk," Rhys informed him.

"Lube in your desk?" Peter asked, raising his eyebrows. "Why would you have lube in your desk?"

"I might need to jack off." Rhys smiled. "I do jack off on occasion."

"Okay, I'll buy that. Hold on a moment, baby. I'll be right back." Peter slapped Rhys's ass.

Rhys wiggled his ass back and forth, smiling over his shoulder as he did. "Oh yeah, baby, slap my ass."

Peter laughed and slapped his ass again before he jogged down the steps into Rhys's office. He glanced at the storyboards and noticed on the third that Rhys really was going for something different. He took a step closer to it and looked at the house that Rhys had sketched out. It looked a lot like the house they were in now.

"Top left drawer, Peter," Rhys called.

Peter turned away from the board and what looked like a murder mystery game to grab the lube from the desk. He hurried back up the stairs and noticed Rhys was exactly as he left him, holding on to the railing and staring out at the yard below.

"Such a beautiful sight," Peter commented, walking up behind Rhys.

"I hope you're talking about me." Rhys smiled over his shoulder at him.

"No sight more beautiful," he whispered, running his hand down his lover's back.

Rhys turned to face him and leaned against the railing. He spread his legs a little so Peter could step between them. Peter stepped closer, his nose running along Rhys's cheek, smelling the man he loved before he gave him a soft kiss. Rhys opened to him, and he slipped his tongue in, tasting the sweetness of his lover. He ran his thumb along Rhys's jawline, chuckling when Rhys turned to nip at it. The move opened Rhys's neck to Peter's mouth. He began to suck, scraping his teeth along the pulse point, moaning when Rhys bit his thumb. He continued to kiss and nip his way along Rhys's smooth neck to move up to his ear, nudging the hair away with his nose to expose it to his tongue. Rhys laughed as Peter dipped his tongue into Rhys's ear, swirling around as Rhys's head jerked away slightly.

Peter bit the delicate earlobe, feeling Rhys shudder under him. He skimmed his nails along the bare skin of Rhys's sides, knowing the sensation would bring goose bumps to Rhys's flesh. Rhys moaned as he wrapped his arms around Peter's shoulders and pulled him close.

Peter began to thrust against Rhys, the friction of their skin making both of their cocks harder. Rhys sat on the railing, his legs locked around Peter's waist.

"Careful, baby," Peter whispered against his skin. "I don't want you to fall."

Rhys looked at the ground below. "It's a little over two stories. I might break something, but it won't kill me, not unless I land on my head."

Peter grabbed his waist and pulled him closer. The new angle pushed Rhys's cock further up, causing more friction.

"Fuck me, Peter," Rhys gasped, reaching blindly along the rail for the lube.

"In a minute," Peter whispered against his cheek.

"I don't have a fucking minute. I want you in me, Peter. I need you in me."

Peter took a step back, pulling Rhys with him. "Turn around and grab the railing. I want to take you as you stand."

Rhys unlocked his legs and let himself down. He turned around, grabbed the railing, and thrust his ass out.

"You really want me, don't you?" Peter squirted a little lube on his fingers and began to run them up and down Rhys's crack before pushing two fingers in the hungry hole.

"Take your fucking jeans off and get that dick up my ass," Rhys growled.

"I might just leave them on, let you feel the rough material on your body, the zipper scratching your ass as I fuck you."

"I don't give a flying fuck either way, as long as it means your cock is buried in my ass." Rhys panted pushing his ass out toward Peter.

Peter stripped out of his jeans, not wanting anything between him and Rhys. He loved the feel of skin on skin, and even though the thought of wearing jeans made the act seem somehow naughty, it wasn't an area he wanted to go to right now.

"I love you, Rhys," Peter whispered.

"I love you too, baby, more than life itself." Rhys looked over his shoulder at Peter lubing up his cock.

Peter took a few extra moments to slide his hand up and down his hard shaft knowing that Rhys was watching the whole time and getting turned on by the process. He reached down between Rhys's legs, spread his cheeks, and let his lubed finger skim over the tight, hot hole.

"Fuck me, baby," Rhys gasped, pressing against the fingers.

"Let me at least get you ready." Peter chuckled.

"Fuck that, give me that awesome cock of yours," Rhys moaned, pushing down against the fingers.

"Damn, you're a horny little fucker, aren't you?" Peter slipped his fingers past the tight ring of muscles and lubed up the entrance. He used two fingers to stretch Rhys. Rhys pushed down on his fingers, matching the thrusting. After a few moments, Peter removed his fingers and lined his cock up. He tried to go slow but Rhys braced his hands on the railing and pushed down, impaling himself on the hard cock. Both men groaned in pleasure, and Rhys's eyes rolled back in his head.

Rhys shoved back as Peter slammed forward, the sound of skin on skin, balls hitting ass loud in the silence of the day. A gentle wind blew across them, cooling their sweat-covered bodies. Peter slammed into Rhys harder and faster. He couldn't remember a time when Rhys seemed to be slamming back so hard. It was almost like Rhys couldn't get Peter's cock hard enough or deep enough.

Peter dug his fingers into Rhys's side, trying to get a better grip on the man. He tried to find a steady rhythm, to slow the pace down a little. Letting go of the railing, Rhys stood, his back pressed against Peter's chest. Peter ran his hands up and down Rhys's chest, pinching the hard nipples as his fingers made contact with them. He ran his fingers down, skimming over Rhys's smooth stomach, and Rhys sucked in his breath as Peter hit a ticklish spot.

Peter moved his hand down further to stroke his hard cock as Rhys reached over his head and locked his fingers behind Peter's head. It wasn't a position that Peter liked really, it didn't give him the depth he preferred, but he did enjoy the closeness, the contact of skin on skin. He thrust up, short shallow thrusts, holding Rhys close as possible to him. Peter bit Rhys's neck, his teeth scraping along the exposed flesh, and Rhys moaned and tilted his head to give Peter better access. Peter matched his strokes to his thrusts, Rhys wiggling back and forth, rubbing his body all over Peter's.

"Turn around, lover. I don't like this position much."

Rhys stepped away, turned to face him, and wrapped his arms back around Peter. He lifted his legs and leaned back so Pete could thrust back in. Peter did just that, his dick ramming back into Rhys's hot ass. It wasn't the best position, as it forced Rhys backward with his back on the railing as Peter brought Rhys's leg up higher for a deeper penetration.

"Fuck, this kind of hurts my back," Rhys panted, digging his nails into Peter's chest and leaving red trails.

"Let's move to the floor." Peter pulled out again, the cool air hitting his cock.

Rhys lay on the floor, grabbed his legs, and pulled them up to his chest. Peter dropped to the ground before him, lined up with the waiting hole and plunged into the hot depths. They both moaned in pleasure as Rhys slid his nails down Peter's back, bringing red scratches to the surface. Peter pushed harder, faster, as if he could somehow pound Rhys though the floor and into the attic below them. He leaned forward, pulling Rhys's legs up higher so he could kiss him. He fucked him hard and fast, the sound of skin hitting skin loud, Peter felt they could hear it all over the yard.

"Oh fuck, Peter!" Rhys screamed, his nails digging into Peter's back.

"I'm close, baby," Peter panted, flinching slightly when Rhys dug into his back again.

"Stroke me, baby," Rhys gasped. He leaned up biting into Peter's shoulder as Peter took Rhys cock and began to pump wildly.

"Oh God, baby," Peter moaned, moving his hand faster up and down Rhys's cock. He put a slight twist in his wrist as he skimmed his hand over the head, a squeeze as his hand came back down.

"Harder!" Rhys screamed out.

"Oh God, baby!" Peter panted, thrusting harder than before. He grabbed Rhys's hands, shoved them above his head, and held him in place.

Rhys tried to impale himself more deeply on Peter's dick.

"Oh fuck, Rhys!" he cried out.

"I'm close, Peter." Rhys reached down, grabbed his balls, and pulled them away from his body. "I'm not ready to come yet, this feels too fucking good."

"I don't know if I can hold off much longer."

"That's fine." Rhys began to work his ass, using his inner sheath to stroke Peter's cock. "I want you to come before me anyway."

Peter dug his fingers into Rhys's wrist, holding Rhys still as he shoved in harder and faster, trying to bring them both at the same time.

"Fuck! Oh fuck! Oh God! Oh! Oh!" Rhys screamed out his words until they became just one long scream.

Peter was right behind him, the waves of his orgasm washing over him until he was nothing more than a bundle of nerves. He was alive, his body feeling everything. He collapsed against Rhys, his breath coming out in ragged gasps.

"Fuck," Rhys said as he brought his arms around Peter's waist and held Peter close.

"I don't think I can move," Peter gasped, still trying to regain his breath.

"Then don't." Rhys lowered his legs until he was a little more comfortable. "This is the perfect moment for me. I love you so much, baby. Promise me you'll always stay with me, you'll always love and protect me."

Peter buried his face into Rhys's neck. "I promise to always take care of you, baby."

"I bit you," Rhys commented.

"Were you trying to mark me so everyone would know that I'm claimed?"

Rhys chuckled. "I guess I want someone to know that you're mine."

Peter closed his eyes, enjoying the feeling of Rhys's breath on his skin and the cool air that blew across them both, and he drifted off to sleep.

Peter walked through the house. He could hear angry voices. Someone was yelling, but he couldn't understand the words. It took him a moment to realize it wasn't English, something more clipped, Russian maybe. He stood at the top of the stairs. The laughter of men came from below.

Peter took a deep breath. He needed to go down the stairs. He placed his hand on the railing and began to take the steps one at a time. The voices continued in the clipped language before the laughter started again.

Peter could feel his skin tingle as the hairs stood on end. He stepped off the last step and turned to look into the front room. The man—what had Alexey called him, Demetri—stood with his back to the stairs. A second man sat in the chair facing Alexey, who stood in the middle of the front room, his hands tied above him. The rope, which was wrapped around a hook in the ceiling, cut into his wrists, leaving angry red marks.

Alexey was looking at Peter, his eyes pleading for help. He stood on his toes, and his body swayed as his legs threatened to give out. His face was tearstained, yet he made no sound.

Demetri walked over to Alexey. He yanked the gag from his mouth, leaned forward, and kissed Alexey, shoving his tongue in. The force of the kiss knocked Alexey off-balance, his weight coming down on his arms.

Demetri walked around behind him.

"Would you protect me?" Alexey asked Peter.

"Of course." Peter tried to move closer, but his feet refused to obey him.

Pain flashed across Alexey's face as Demetri roughly began to fuck him.

"It would never hurt with you," Alexey whispered. "It never hurts with you."

Peter shook his head. "Never. Sex is magical, something shared between two people in love. It should never hurt."

Alexey closed his eyes for a moment, a small smile on his lips. "You would love me if Rhys wasn't here, wouldn't you?"

"Rhys?" Peter looked confused. "Alexey, I'd have taken care of you even if Rhys was here. I wouldn't ever have let that sadistic bastard touch you, hurt you, fuck you, or anything else for that matter. Rhys would have helped protect you just like I would have."

Alexey shook his head for a moment. "Rhys won't let me have you, but he'll change his mind, you wait and see."

"What?" Peter asked, confused by what Alexey said.

The man who had been watching suddenly stood up. He grabbed a cane off the table, moved to stand in front of Alexey, and tested the flexibility. Alexey stared at Peter, his eyes slowly closing in anticipation. The man drew his arm back. Peter could swear he almost heard it slice through the air.

"No!" Peter screamed.

Peter awoke with a jerk, momentarily unsure where he was. A cool breeze drifted over his body and brought forth a shudder. He reached up to rub the sleep from his eyes as the last remnants of the dream faded, and the realization that they were still on the roof came back to him.

"Wake up, Rhys baby." He gently nudged his lover. "We fell asleep on the roof."

"What?" Rhys cracked one eye open. "What the fuck are we doing on the roof?"

Peter sat up. "You dragged me up here for sex, remember?"

Rhys looked around for his clothes. "Not really. Damn I'm fucking sore. What the hell did you do to me?"

"Me do to you?" Peter gasped in shock. "I'm the one who has scratches on his back. You moaned and screamed and begged me to do it harder, to pound you through the roof."

Rhys stood there for a moment, his clothes clutched against his chest. "Through the roof? Let me tell you, my ass is sore enough that it feels like you tried to pound me through the roof or used your dick to pin me to the floor of the widow's walk."

Peter picked up his own clothes. "You really don't remember dragging me up here?"

Rhys gave a sigh, shaking his head as he started back down the steps. "I've almost finished the game. It's in trials now. I have ideas I need to get down for the sequel. Sex is the furthest thing from my mind."

Peter stared at Rhys as he walked down the steps. Shaking his head, Peter trotted down the steps after Rhys. "What do you mean you don't remember dragging me upstairs?"

Rhys pulled his clothes on. "That's what I said. I don't remember dragging you upstairs. I'm not saying I didn't. Hell, I don't remember having sex with you. My body and my ass say we did, and I can't remember the last time I've been so sore after sex, but I honestly don't remember any of it."

Peter pulled his jeans on. "What's happening to us, Rhys?"

Rhys shook his head, his trembling hands running through his hair. "I honestly don't know."

Peter dropped the rest of his clothes on the floor. He walked over and slid his arms around Rhys's waist. Rhys turned in his arms and snuggled close.

"It'll be okay, Rhys. We'll figure this all out."

Rhys kissed his cheek, but Peter could feel the dampness of the tears that filled Rhys's eyes. "As long as you love me, we can get through anything."

"Always and forever, baby."

Chapter 19

RHYS SHUT down his computer. The game had a couple of glitches, something he hadn't noticed before it went out to the beta tester. It wasn't hard to fix, but it was tedious all the same. Shoving his hair out of his eyes, he pushed the chair away from the computer. He needed to take a break from the game. He grabbed his empty water bottle from his desk and started down the stairs.

Rhys could see the light on in Peter's office. He thought about stopping in for a moment, but if Peter was finally able to get something down, he didn't want to interrupt him. He jogged down the second flight of steps, feeling really good about the work he was getting done. His stomach rumbled, reminding him he needed to eat. Rhys glanced out the french doors and noticed just how beautiful of a day it was. When he got back to his office, he would have to open the door that led to the roof, let a little fresh air and sunlight in. He was surprised that Peter wasn't outside right now.

He walked across the living room, not noticing the pair of shoes that lay in the middle of the room until he tripped over them. He felt himself start to fall, and the more he tried to catch his balance, the more entangled his feet became. He stuck his hands out hoping to break his fall as his forehead hit the wall. Rhys sat on the floor, momentarily stunned. He felt light-headed; his vision began to fade as the darkness engulfed him.

"WHAT DO you need, babe?" Peter looked up from his computer to see Rhys standing in the doorway.

Rhys continued to stare at him, not moving, not acknowledging he had spoken.

"Rhys, babe?" Peter slid his chair back.

"What do you want for lunch?"

"Are you okay, babe? You don't sound like yourself." Peter stood.

"I'm fine."

Peter walked across the room, and his hand instinctively went to Rhys's cheek.

"I'm sorry I disturbed you."

"It's okay, baby. I needed a break anyway." Peter gave him a quick kiss.

Rhys breathed in sharply, his mouth opening for more. Peter slid his tongue into the warm inviting mouth, tasting, exploring, and caressing the soft tongue. His arms went around his lover and held him close. Rhys stood still, his hands at his side as if he wasn't sure what to do with them.

Peter pulled away a little, his nose nudging Rhys's before he dipped back in for another kiss, his tongue parting the lips, his hands running caressing Rhys's back.

He felt Rhys's arms go around him as he leaned into the kiss. His whole body seemed to melt into the kiss as Rhys's hand slid down to cup his ass.

"We shouldn't, Rhys. I need to get this story ready for line edits, and you need to get the last glitches out of the game."

"Later?" Rhys whispered, barely pulling away.

Peter placed his face in Rhys's neck, smelling his lover. Sometimes he loved just holding Rhys, to let his calm nature fix everything that was right in his world.

"I love you, Rhys, I really do, but we both have deadlines. If you could just wait until this evening, I would be more than happy to show you just how much I love you."

"Do you promise?" Rhys whispered.

Peter kissed his jawline. "I promise."

Rhys leaned into him, his eyes closed as he gave a soft contented sigh.

Peter held him a few moments longer, enjoying the way he felt, the way he smelled.

"What did you need, Peter?"

Peter took a step away from him. "What do you mean? You came in here to me."

Rhys looked around the room. "I don't remember coming in here. I remember jogging downstairs. I planned on grabbing something to eat and more water. I know I was thinking about how nice it looked outside and wondering why you weren't outside. I was thinking that I needed to show you my game to see what you thought about it."

"Do you want to do that now?" Peter offered. "Show me your game?"

Rhys pushed his hair out of his eyes, and sighing deeply, he looked past Peter to the open window. "Fuck, I hate that I can't remember coming in here."

Peter placed his hands on either side of Rhys's face. Holding the man still, he leaned in to give him a good firm kiss. "You were thinking about your game. That's why you can't remember coming in here. Don't stress over it, okay? You keep telling me that everything I think I hear and see is stress. I'm sure it's the same with you."

Rhys nodded, but he didn't act like he really believed it. "It sounds really bad when you put it that way."

"Come on, let's go to your office and check out the video game." He took Rhys's hand and pulled him from the office into the hallway.

"Yeah, let's look at my game. Tell me your honest opinion, though. I had to make a couple big changes when it came back from the beta testers, so let me know if it all flows."

Peter laughed as he opened the door to Rhys's office. "You say that like I would be able to remotely play your video games. Hell, I think those marked five and under are too hard for me."

Rhys laughed, some of the tension leaving his body. "Fine, I'll play it for you, but let me know what you think of the graphics."

"I'm sure those are going to be awesome and lifelike." Peter squeezed his hand as they walked up the stairs and into Rhys's office. "You know the one that had those giant spiders gave me bad dreams for days."

"No giant spiders," Rhys assured him. "A few zombies, but no spiders."

Peter stood behind Rhys as he took a seat and loaded the game. The graphics were unbelievable. It always amazed Peter how real the video games looked. He watched as Rhys moved through the game shooting zombies, the blood flying rather convincingly in his opinion. He really had no idea what the blood spatter looked like when you shot someone, but he was pretty sure it was realistic looking.

Peter began to absently play with a lock of his lover's hair, looking at the video game that Rhys was playing.

"What do you think so far?" Rhys asked.

"It looks good. Are you done with it?" Peter rubbed his shoulders.

"No." He sighed turning off the computer. "It still has a few glitches in it."

"I think from the looks, though, that people won't mind lining up at midnight to get the copy the moment it goes on sale."

"I can't believe I have a midnight release." He turned to look at Peter, his smile huge.

"Yeah, you have an actual deadline, so you better get the last few glitches out of it. I hope someday one of my books is popular enough to get a midnight release."

"It'll happen soon enough, baby. Until then, you make a good steady income, and I think that is more important."

"You're right." Peter sighed as he sat in the chair beside Rhys. "I'd rather have a steady income and a loyal following."

"Believe me, when you get a couple of bestsellers, people expect you to do it every time. They're much more critical of your work, take it from the gamer."

Peter gave him a quick kiss. "I agree. I don't want the pressure you're under right now."

"It's probably why I've been so spacey lately." Rhys turned his chair to face Peter. "I can't believe I'm bumping into things, sleepwalking, and just spacing out in general."

"Do you want to go to town and grab a pizza or something?" Peter kissed him again.

"Yeah, I need to take a break from this. I'm going to miss a glitch or two if I don't. Let me close this all out, and I'll be down."

"Okay, I'll be downstairs."

Rhys nodded as he began to close down his game. "I'm going to run a comb through my hair, and I'll be there."

Peter gave Rhys a quick kiss before he headed out of the office and down the steps to the second story. He heard Rhys shut the office door and start down the steps behind him. He turned, jogged down the steps to the first floor, and crossed the front room to turn on the lamp. He wasn't sure they would be back before dark and really hated to come back to a dark home. He always felt like a blind man, his hands out before him, groping the wall for the light switch.

"Rhys, are you coming or not?" Peter called up the stairs. He reached in his pocket and felt for his car keys.

"I'll be just a moment more." Rhys walked to the top of the stairs. "Let me finish my hair, and I'll be down."

"Do you know where my car keys are?"

"I put them in the bowl on the table." Rhys headed back into the bathroom.

"Thanks, honey." Peter walked to the small table that Rhys had set by the front door. His car keys were in the dish.

"You left them sitting on the kitchen counter." Rhys started down the stairs. "You really need to start putting them in the dish the moment you get home."

"I know." Peter shoved them in his pocket and turned to watch Rhys.

Rhys walked slowly, checking the messages on his phone. Suddenly he began to stumble, his phone bouncing on the steps, his hands grabbing for something to stop the fall but connecting with nothing.

"Rhys!" Peter ran across the room and came to a stop in front of the prone man.

"I felt like I was pushed." Rhys allowed Peter to help him up as he gingerly tested his foot.

"Pushed?" Peter helped him across the room to the couch. "Let me take a look at your ankle."

Rhys slid back a little as Peter took off his shoe. "I was walking down the stairs, and I felt a hand in the middle of my back. I know what I felt, Peter."

"I don't think it's broken, but we can take you to the doctor if you want."

He shook his head. "I'm fine, just a little sore."

"You know you and I are the only two here, Rhys. Who could have pushed you?"

Rhys lay back on the couch, his eyes closed. "I don't know, Peter. I don't know what's wrong with me. I don't know why I've been having little accidents and forgetting time, sleepwalking, or anything else like that. I know it felt like I was pushed. Maybe the house *is* haunted, and I am the one that it picks on. I don't know why this stuff is happening, but it is, I can't deny it any longer."

Peter gave a soft sigh. "You honestly believe I'm right and the house is haunted?"

"Don't fucking patronize me, Peter. I know I've given you a hard time about believing in ghosts."

"I'm not, Rhys, I promise you I'm not." Peter ran his hands through his hair. "I kept telling myself that it was the stress. I've heard voices, Rhys. I hear this whispering, and then I hear sobbing. I don't know how many times I hear it, but…."

Rhys reached for Peter and pulled him close. "But the broken vase, the doors opening, what sounds like a window slamming, the water being turned on, me feeling like someone is trying to take over my body, and now I was pushed. We can't ignore it any longer, Peter. Something wants us out of this house."

"Maybe it just wants help?" Peter suggested. "I hear crying, and the dreams I have all tie into it. What if Alexey wants help?"

Rhys rolled his eyes. "I think we need to get someone out here to cleanse the house or some crap. This ghost doesn't want help, Peter, unless it's help getting us the fuck out."

Peter shrugged. "I've seen it on TV. Once they are laid to rest, they move on."

"How do you know his name is Alexey? We've asked around, you've done research. There has never been an Alexey, Peter."

"The dreams, the whispers in the woods." Peter looked at Rhys's ankle again. "Maybe we should just forget it and leave. Alexey has been making threats to hurt you and now it seems he has enough energy to push you down a flight of stairs."

"What about the money we've spent on the house?" Rhys asked, reaching forward to take hold of Peter's hand. "It took a large part of our savings to buy this."

"The attacks are aimed at you. Don't ask me how, but I know it. I'd rather lose the house and everything with it than stay here where you could get hurt. This stuff...." He gestured around him. "They're objects. You're the one I love, and if anything happened to you, I'd die."

Rhys gave him a kiss. "I love you too. I talked you into this house. Let's see if we can find out anything about the Alexey before we run screaming. If he was in this country there is information about him somewhere. If we had an idea what year he came to America we could see if Demetri entered with a guest, or find his immigration papers or something."

"One more thing happens to you in this house, and I'll toss you over my shoulder and carry you out of here, you understand?"

Rhys smiled. "I like it when you get all caveman on me."

"So do you want me to be a caveman or a caring husband as I help you to the bedroom?"

Rhys wrapped his arms around Peter's neck. "As much as I'd like you to be all caveman. I think you would end up with a hernia if you tried to carry me up a flight of stairs."

"You might be surprised. I've been lifting weights." He reached down and lifted Rhys off the couch.

"Honest, baby, you're going to strain something." Rhys wrapped his arms tighter around Peter's neck.

"So little faith." Peter crossed the room to the stairs. "See, I got you this far."

"Can't get me up the stairs, can you?"

Peter looked up the flight of stairs. "No, I can't."

Rhys laughed out loud as Peter set him on his feet. "It was a wonderful gesture, though."

"Put your weight on me, and I'll help you upstairs."

Rhys leaned against Peter, his other hand on the railing as they made their way up the stairs.

"When you feel better, we'll go back to the local library and see if we can find anything on the history of the house. We can look at the old newspapers and see if there were any deaths or murders here."

"Wait a moment." Rhys stopped them as they made it to the top of the stairs. "I'm not in as good of shape as I thought I was. Maybe I need to soak my foot. Could you run me a nice hot bath?"

"Sure, baby." Peter helped him into the bathroom making sure Rhys was comfortable on the stool. Peter turned on the water. "Do you want me to put bubbles in it?"

Rhys shook his head. "I just want to sit on the edge and soak my foot in the water."

"Well, actually you're supposed to put your ankle in cold water. Why not let me run you a nice bubble bath, and you can soak your ankle and the rest of your body. You fell down a bunch of steps, sweetie. Your whole body could be hurting soon."

"Ah hell, why not? Put some salts in the water, a ton of bubble bath, and I'll soak the bruises away from my body."

Peter walked back over to Rhys and trailed his fingers along his jawline. He felt Rhys leaned into his hand. "I love you, Rhys. It would kill me if anything ever happened to you."

"Then you better never let anything happen to me."

"Tomorrow we are going into town. I don't care if I have to spend all fucking day in the library looking through every piece of paper this town produced. I'm going to find out what happened here. No one hurts my baby, and no one will run us out of our house."

Chapter 20

"WHAT IS all this stuff?" Rhys asked as Peter set the bags on the table.

"You said we should start investigating our own house. While you were working on the game, I decided to drive into town and see what I could find. I have to admit, there wasn't a lot but it's a start."

Rhys began to shuffle through the bags. "Digital recorders?"

"So the ghost can talk to us, and a camera to take its picture."

"The rest of the stuff?"

"Well okay, the rest of the stuff is for us. I was in a shopping mood, and I bought a bunch of crap that we don't really need." Peter smiled as he pulled the items out of the bag.

"It looks like you were in a chocolate mood also." Rhys held up the brownie mix, then the candy bars, then the double-chocolate-chip cookies. "Or is it just a sugar mood? I'm already getting a few love handles. I don't need you to make it a love tire."

Peter reached over to pat Rhys's stomach. "Love handles just mean there is more of you to hold onto as I fuck you senseless."

"Funny." Rhys grabbed up the sugary sweets and carried them to the kitchen.

"Wait a sec, Rhys." Peter fished through the bag.

Rhys stopped in the doorway.

"I also got chocolate chips to add to the brownies." He tossed the bag to Rhys, who caught it one-handed.

"I'll make them this afternoon, okay, sweetie?"

"Great. When you get those put away, we will start our ghost investigation."

Rhys shook his head as he walked into the kitchen and let the door swing behind him.

Peter opened his devices and checked them over to see where the batteries went. He was pretty sure he had enough batteries. He had spent the extra money to get the really good ones. After all, a ghost needed the energy to appear. He pushed the Play button to make sure it was working. When he was satisfied with the results, he opened the camera box.

"Are you sure you want to do this?" Rhys asked, walking back into the dining room.

"We need to find out what Alexey wants and how to help him move on." He snapped a few pictures around the room to test the camera.

"I feel like a freaking idiot," Rhys muttered as Peter handed him the digital recorder.

"All the ghost shows use digital recorders to see who's haunting their house. We will be no different," Peter countered.

"Then you can walk around talking out loud." He thrust it back into Peter's hands.

"Fine." Peter rolled his eyes at Rhys. "I think you have the better speaking voice, but if you won't do it, I will."

"I'm pretty damn sure that if the house is haunted, they won't care that much about your enunciation."

Peter switched on the recorder. "Hello? Is anyone here?"

"You and me," Rhys whispered.

"Do you have a name? Can we help you any?"

"I thought you said his name was Alexey," Rhys muttered under his breath.

"Would you shut up? How can I find out what the ghost needs with your running commentary?" Peter glared at him.

Rhys made a motion of zipping his lips.

"Good." Peter turned his attention back to what he was doing. He began to walk around the house. "Alexey? Are you here?"

He paused, giving Alexey time to answer. "How can I help you, Alexey? Do you need me to finish some business for you? What is your last name? Who was Demetri? Was he your boyfriend?"

"Do you honestly think you're going to get a response?"

"You know, Rhys, if you're going to be so negative, maybe you should just wait in the other room."

"I'm sorry, Peter." Rhys hugged him, his chin resting on Peter's shoulder. "I'll be more supportive, I promise. Let's find out who is haunting our house and why."

Peter leaned back against Rhys, enjoying the support of Rhys's arms for a moment before stepping away and continuing with the investigation.

"What do you want, Alexey? Why are you haunting our house?" He continued asking questions.

"Is there a room that you like to be in more than the others?" He started up the stairs.

Rhys followed close behind, snapping pictures as he went. "I'm wondering if I'll get a picture of a ghost smiling at me."

"Rhys!"

"Yeah, you're right. He'll probably be giving me the finger."

Peter stopped and turned to face Rhys. He couldn't keep the glare off his face.

"Fine, Peter." Rhys managed to look a little sheepish.

They continued to walk through the house, Peter stopping in each room to ask questions while Rhys snapped pictures.

"On the bright side, we will have plenty of pictures of the interior of the house."

"Rhys!" Peter threw his hands in the air. "Why the hell am I even bothering? You said you were on board with this whole idea. I expected you to be supportive."

"I'm sorry, baby." Rhys pulled Peter into his arms and gave him a kiss on the forehead. "I'll be good."

"Forget it." Peter walked toward the stairs, his shoulders slumped in defeat. If Rhys wasn't going to do anything more than make fun of the whole thing, then Peter would do it when he wasn't around.

"Come on, Peter, don't be that way." Rhys started to follow him. "Why don't we go listen to what we have? Maybe you caught something."

"No, I don't want to listen to it with you, not if you're going to make fun of the whole thing."

Rhys grabbed Peter's shoulder and turned him around. "Stop, Peter. I'm really sorry, all right. I'm just scared and this is how I deal with it. You know I can't help but be sarcastic when I'm scared, especially if I can't just hide behind you. You've always been my protector, my knight in slightly tarnished armor, and this time you're just as scared as I am."

Peter nodded, the anger leaving his body. "I'm sorry too, baby. I just don't know what to do. I've always had the answers. I've always protected you and now…."

Rhys leaned in for a kiss and brushed his lips lightly over Peter's. "You're still my protector, Peter. I still want to curl up in your arms at night and have you make everything better for me."

"What if I can't this time, Rhys?" He glanced down at the recorder in Rhys's hand. "What do we do then? We can't let things go on like this. I feel like I'm going crazy. You're getting pushed, having moments when you black out. What happens next? How can I protect you from something I can't see?"

"Are you ready to listen to this?" Rhys handed Peter the recorder.

"Sort of."

"Sort of?" Rhys asked, sitting on the couch beside him. "I thought you couldn't wait to find out who was in our house. You couldn't wait to find out if your dream man was trying to connect with you."

Peter nodded, his finger running up and down the smooth silver cover of the recorder. "I do. I'm just afraid there is going to be nothing there."

Rhys ran the back of his hand over Peter's cheek. "It doesn't mean there is nothing in the house. It just means we didn't get anything this time."

"I'm more afraid there will be a voice there." Peter turned to look at him.

"Wouldn't that give you the validation you desire, to finally be able to say I was right?"

Peter nodded, taking a deep breath. "The dreams are terrible, Rhys. I hate to think that Alexey suffered and died here. I hate to think no one cared enough to try and help him. I hate to think he's been forgotten by everyone."

"Someone cares enough now, and that's what's important."

Peter closed his eyes. He was ready for this, he really was, no matter what he heard on the tape. He took a deep breath to steel his nerves. Opening his eyes, he looked at Rhys, the calm smiling Rhys. When had Rhys become his rock? Peter had always taken care of them both. He was the strong protector, but somehow now Rhys had taken the role of protector. Rhys with his calm gentle ways—it felt really good to be able to lean on him for emotional support.

"Are you ready for this, Peter?" He took the recorder from Peter's hands.

"I love you, Rhys. Thank you for standing by me even though I may be going absolutely batshit crazy."

Rhys laughed. "Well, even if you are batshit crazy, you're still the sexiest man I know. Besides, I think I promised to love you for all my days. I meant it then, and I mean it now."

"Let's get this over with. The sooner we find out if there is a voice on the recorder, the sooner we can help Alexey move on."

Rhys pushed Play. Peter's voice seemed rather loud as he asked questions. They waited, straining their ears to hear a voice in the static. The questions came one after the other, but there was no voice to answer the questions. Peter closed his eyes. There was no voice. There was no proof he wasn't making it all up. Rhys had believed him for a while, but now....

"*Alexey, do you need help?*" His voice came through the tiny speaker.

"*Help*" came the whispered reply.

Peter sat up straighter, he grabbed for the recorder. After pushing Rewind, he listened again.

"*Alexey, do you need help?*"

"*Help.*"

"Did you hear that?" Peter turned the recorder off and looked at Rhys.

"I heard. Let's see if anything else is captured." Rhys turned the recorder back on.

"*How can we help you, Alexey?*"

"*Protect me.*"

"*What do you want, Alexey? How can we help you?*"

"*You promised.*"

"*What do you want, Alexey?*"

"*To live.*"

"*How can we help, Alexey?*"

"*Peter, please, Peter.*"

Peter turned the recorder off, a cold, fine sweat covering his body. "Did you hear that?"

Rhys was pale. "I'm sorry I didn't believe you, Peter."

"What does he mean, 'to live'?"

"What does he mean about you promising him something? What was it you promised?" Rhys asked him.

"To protect him," Peter murmured. "Do you think Demetri killed him and buried him here somewhere?"

"There are so many places Demetri could have buried him. We have three hundred acres, Peter. I wouldn't even know where to look."

Peter looked at the recorder in his hand. "Maybe he will answer it later? We didn't ask the question of where he was buried. Maybe next time we can."

"Next time?" Rhys cocked one eyebrow. "I think one time was enough for me."

"It's that, or walk over every inch of this land looking for a sign that says body buried here."

"No one likes a smartass, Peter."

Peter stood and looked at the recorder, then at Rhys. He ran his hands over his face before he began to pace back and forth. "I wish I knew where to turn, where to look for help."

"Now you know you're not going batshit crazy. You're the writer, Peter. You have to do the research. You have better ideas where to look than I ever will."

Peter thought about that for a moment. "Well, I guess I'd start with Demetri. He came from the Soviet Union, at least the papers and Internet said he did. He had to have a visa or a passport or something like that. We also know he bought the house in the '30s. I can look at records from the sale and see if I can get a little more information there."

"Okay, that's a start." Rhys took his hand and ran small circles with his thumb on the back of it.

"So maybe Alexey had a passport or something also, assuming he came from the same area. The librarian said Demetri lived in the house a good sixty years, so I start looking at immigration records before then. I found Demetri's obituary, but it didn't list family. In fact none of the articles I read about him listed a family. Maybe what I need to do is look at all immigrations records from 1939-1941. I can see if anyone named Alexey or some variation of that entered America at that time. Maybe I can find out if Demetri sponsored Alexey. Then again, with so many Jewish people fleeing Europe and coming to America during that time, he might have gotten lost in the shuffle. It's a place to look, though. Of course, that's going to take time."

"Sounds like you have a plan."

"I need to go to the library, maybe the librarian will be able to help me with the research. There is always a chance she will remember something, perhaps she saw Alexey once and just doesn't remember it. Do you want to come?"

Rhys shook his head. "I've got a couple of things I need to do here."

"Are you sure you want to be alone in the house?" Peter asked him. "Are you sure you're going to be safe?"

Rhys looked around. "I can't be afraid of my own house, Peter."

Peter kissed his forehead. "I love you more than life itself."

Rhys rested his forehead against Peter's. "I love you too, baby."

Chapter 21

"IT LOOKS like a storm is coming in," Peter commented as he watched the news.

"It's not all that close. There is still a chance it might pass us by." Rhys shrugged, looking from the TV to the windows. "I can see stars."

"It would be coming in from the other side, sweetie." Pete laughed. He kissed Rhys's cheek and snuggled him close. "Don't worry, though, I can think of a few ways to distract you from the storm."

Rhys rolled his eyes. He got up from the couch and stood looking down at Peter. "I think I'm going to take a bath. Do you want to join me?"

Peter held up a book. "I'm fine. You go ahead and take a nice relaxing bath without me molesting you."

Rhys stared at Peter, then reached out and felt Peter's forehead. "Are you sick? I can't think of a time you have turned down a chance to fondle me."

Peter took Rhys's hand, brought it down from his forehead, and kissed the palm of his hand. "Take your bath, baby. Put lots of bubbles in it, and I'll let you relax."

Rhys shook his head. "You don't know what you're missing. I'm sexy as hell when I'm all wet and soapy."

Peter looked him up and down. "Yeah, I do, but I'll be seeing it soon. I can almost guarantee you will be all wet and sexy when you snuggle close to me telling me to keep you warm."

"Suit yourself." Rhys turned around. Shaking his ass in Peter's face, he sashayed toward the stairs.

"Keep shaking your ass like that, though, and I may change my mind."

Rhys slapped his own ass. "You know where it will be when you decide you want it."

Peter chuckled. He slid down the couch a little until he was comfortable, then opened his book. "Later, baby doll."

Rhys shook his head as he walked toward the stairs.

Peter started to read. He really wanted to finish this book. It was by one of his favorite authors, but for some reason he had problems getting into this book. His eyes itched, so he closed them for just a moment and drifted quickly off to sleep.

"I want you to get rid of Rhys." Alexey slid up to Peter. "He's in the way, Peter darling. He keeps us apart."

"Us?" Peter took a step back from Alexey. "What do you mean 'us'?"

"Us, Peter. You said you would love and protect me. You can't do that with Rhys here. I know you want to spend more time with me, but he keeps getting in the way. Send him away, Peter."

"Alexey, I married Rhys. I love him. Do you understand that?" Peter tried to reason with him.

"I understand that if he wasn't here, you and I could be together. You would have loved me more than you love him. I know you will be happy with me."

"I don't understand what you're saying. How can I be happy with you? This is just a dream. You aren't real."

"Not real?" Alexey's dark eyes flashed with anger. "Just a dream? Is that all I am to you, a fucking dream?"

"I've looked for information on you everywhere, Alexey, and no one knows you.

"My name is Alexey Sergi Jurek. I was born on October 27, 1917. I am no fucking dream!"

"Alexey," Peter sighed.

"In the attic, under the floor boards closest to the east wall there is a picture of me hidden in a tin box. You will find it along with a few other small things if you pry up the floor. You tell me then that I am nothing but a dream to you!"

"Why couldn't you have told me this weeks ago?"

"Get rid of him, Peter!" Alexey screamed.

"I'm not going to get rid of him, Alexey."

Alexey's eyes narrowed. "Then I will."

RHYS SANK down into the hot water, the bubbles covering his body and coming up to his chin. He lay back with his eyes closed as the hot water took all the tension away. Using his toe, he reached up and turned off the water.

He reached for the washcloth, wrung out the water, and placed the cloth over his eyes. Sighing deeply he relaxed, the images of his game running through his mind. He took a deep breath and let it out slowly as he willed the images of the game out of his head. He ran his hand up and down his chest, enjoying the way his fingers felt as they trailed over his wet skin. He rubbed the back of his neck, feeling the tension leave his shoulders as he did. The hot water felt so good. He was glad now that Peter hadn't joined him. He wouldn't have been able to relax this completely with Peter here. He was just drifting off to sleep when he felt something touch him.

Rhys's eyes flew open, and he snatched the cloth off his eyes as unseen hands grabbed his feet and jerked him under the water. Rhys grabbed for the edge of the tub, trying desperately to pull himself up. His hands slipped off the edge as his feet were pulled higher up. He twisted and turned, his fist slamming into the edge of the tub, hoping Peter would hear him struggling. His lungs ached, desperate for air. He tried to grab for the edge of the tub again, but his hands continued to slip on the wet marble. He could feel his vision fading, his lungs begging for air. He hit the side of the tub open-handed, and his last thought was how much he loved Peter.

175

PETER AWOKE with a start, the last traces of the dream leaving his fuzzy mind. Alexey had threatened to hurt Rhys.

"Rhys?" he called, sitting up on the couch. "Rhys, baby?"

He couldn't shake the feeling that Alexey was going to try something. Outside the thunder rumbled as the rain began to fall. He could feel the panic start to form. He headed for the stairs.

"Rhys, baby, answer me!" he called, taking the stairs two at a time, cold fear settling in the pit of his stomach. "Alexey, you better not hurt him!"

Peter ran down the hall to their bedroom. The room was empty, the bathroom door open. Peter could see the water all over the floor. Rhys would never leave a wet floor. Hell, he made sure he wiped up the floor anytime he walked from the tub to the sink.

Peter moved slowly to the bathroom, his heart beating so fast he was sure it could be heard above the rain hitting the window. Thunder rumbled as lightning tore across the sky. He stepped into the bathroom and looked in the tub. It was full of water, but Rhys was nowhere to be seen. He let out the breath he hadn't known he was holding.

He turned and ran through the bedroom and down the hall to push open each door and check the rooms.

"Alexey, if you hurt him, I'll never forgive you. I'll never love you." Peter warned, unsure if Alexey would take his threat seriously.

Peter stood still a moment, hoping Alexey would answer him. When no answer came he started up the stairs to the attic, the one room Rhys might still be in. He walked slower this time. Rhys never liked thunderstorms—the lightning frightened him. Peter could count on Rhys waking him up anytime a storm came at night. He would snuggle into Peter's arms, his face buried in his neck until the storm passed. Peter knew Rhys would never be in the attic alone while a storm raged outside.

"Rhys?" He pushed the door open. The light was on, the room empty. The door that led to the widow's walk stood wide open, the rain blowing in.

"Rhys!" Peter cried out, running for the open door. "Alexey, you better not hurt him!"

He stepped out onto the widow's walk. The lightning flashed overhead, the thunder so loud Peter could almost swear he felt the house shake. The rain fell in sheets soaking him through almost instantly. He could see Rhys sitting on the railing that went around the walk.

"Alexey, no!" Peter screamed, the driving rain plastering his hair to his face.

Rhys turned his head slowly, stiffly. *"I want to be with you, Peter. I can have this body when he's gone."*

Peter took a step closer, then another one, the lightning overhead flashing. "I love Rhys."

"You'll see. You will be happy with me, Peter." Rhys stood, then, leaning over the ledge he held onto the railing with one hand. He looked at Peter, all the love he felt on his face.

Peter moved closer. He held one hand out toward Rhys and used the other to shove the rain-soaked hair back from his face. "How can I be happy if the man I love is dead?"

"You'll love me, wait and see," Alexey whispered as he stepped off the roof.

Peter lunged, grabbing Rhys's hand, the dead weight pulling him off the roof also. He grabbed the railing and held on tight to Rhys.

"What are you doing?" Alexey looked at him through Rhys's eyes.

"If he goes, I go," Peter called down. "Rhys, help me. You have to help, Rhys. I don't know how much longer I can hold on."

Something flickered in Rhys's eyes, a small moment of recognition. "Peter?"

"Help me, Rhys," Peter sobbed, his grip slipping on the metal railing that surrounded the widow's walk.

"Just let me go. Save yourself, Peter. I love you. I have since the first day you ordered coffee from me."

The storm raged, and lightning tore across the sky. The rain blinded Peter, and he desperately wanted to wipe the water from his face. His grip was slipping, both on the railing and on Rhys's hand. Rhys loved him. Rhys trusted him.

"Let me go, Peter," Rhys repeated.

"I love you too, baby," Peter whispered.

"Let me go, Peter. It's okay." The rain mingled with the tears that slid down his face.

"Never." Peter made the decision. He loved Rhys more than anything, and no one would ever take the man from him. Taking a deep breath, he let go of the railing.

They fell and hit the muddy ground with a thud. Peter lay there a moment, stunned, his breath knocked from his body. Giving a groan, he sat up. Nothing seemed to be broken, but he was going to have a hell of a bruise in the morning. He pushed his rain-slicked hair off his face as he turned to look at Rhys.

"Baby?" He patted Rhys's face. "Please wake up, Rhys."

A strange light rose from Rhys's body. Peter pushed himself back as the light hovered for a moment.

"Rhys?" Peter scooted back to Rhys's side, careful not to take his eyes off the blue haze.

"*I just want to be loved.*" The blue haze took the shape of Alexey. "*Why couldn't you love me?*"

"Because you aren't alive." Peter pulled Rhys into his lap as if he could protect him.

"*I could be. If you would have let him die, I could have his body and you could love me.*"

"No, Alexey. You can't take his life in exchange for yours. It's not fair to Rhys."

"*I want to live!*" Alexey screamed before disappearing into the night.

"Wake up, Rhys." Peter patted his face.

Slowly Rhys opened his eyes. "Peter?"

"Oh God, Rhys, you're alive. Are you okay? Is anything broken?"

Rhys lay there a moment. "I don't think so. I don't know."

Peter stood. He reached down and lifted Rhys into his arms, staggering a little under the weight.

"I really should think about dieting." Rhys tried to make light of the situation.

"I've got you, Rhys, I'll never drop you, and I'll never let you go."

"Oh God, Peter." Rhys buried his face in Peter's neck and began to cry. "Why does he want to hurt me?"

"I don't know, baby, but I won't let him hurt you ever again." Peter walked across the yard and headed for the back door. "I'm going to end this tonight."

"No, Peter, let's just leave. Alexey can keep his stupid house."

Peter opened the back door. "No, Rhys. He is not running us out of our house. I worked too hard to make it ours. You made me polish too much damn wood to leave now."

Rhys managed to laugh between the tears.

"He won't drive us out of our house. I refuse to let him." He set Rhys gently on the couch. "You stay right here. I'm going to find Alexey."

"Peter." Rhys grabbed his hand and refused to let him go. "Stay, let's just deal with Alexey later."

"I love you, Rhys, more than anything." Peter gently pushed Rhys's wet hair out of his face.

"I love you too." Rhys turned to kiss the palm of Peter's hand.

"*It's not fair!*" The voice echoed through the house.

"Alexey?" Peter called. "Come on, Alexey, let's talk."

A blue haze appeared in the middle of the room. It shifted and turned until it took the shape of Alexey.

"Alexey, please." Peter let go of Rhys and started walking toward the apparition.

"*You said you loved me!*" Alexey screamed, rushing forward.

Peter stumbled back as the cold wind rushed through his body. He looked at Rhys, who still lay on the couch, his eyes wide as saucers, his skin pale as a ghost.

"Stay here, Rhys. I'm going to find Alexey."

"Peter, be careful."

Peter gave him a quick kiss. "This ends tonight."

"Stay with me Peter."

"I'll be back in a moment." He eased out of Rhys's arms. "He won't hurt me."

Rhys nodded, watching as Peter walked out of the room.

"Alexey? Come on, baby, show yourself to me." He stood in the kitchen turning a slow circle.

Somewhere above him he heard a thump.

"I think he's upstairs," Rhys called from the other room.

"I heard." Peter walked out of the kitchen and headed through the dining room toward the stairs.

"Alexey?" he called as he started up the stairs. "Come on, baby, let's talk. We can work something out."

"*It's not fair!*" Alexey screamed.

"Alexey, where are you?" Peter peered into the front bedroom. Alexey had been in there—the bed sheet lay tossed to the floor, and the mattress stood on its side.

"*I want to live!*"

Peter spun around as doors began to slam shut.

"You should have been given a chance to live. What happened to you wasn't fair." Peter tried to reason with him.

"*You should protect me!*"

Peter noticed a blue light coming from the bathroom. Slowly, cautiously, he moved toward the doorway. Alexey was in the bathroom, kneeling on the floor.

"I would have, if I could have." Peter reached out toward Alexey.

"*Why don't you want me?*" Alexey sobbed. "*Why doesn't anyone want me?*"

"I don't know why Demetri did what he did. I don't know why he didn't love you."

"*Here is where it happened.*" Alexey looked around the room. "*He had beaten me again because I didn't want to have sex with his friends.*"

Peter sat on the floor across from Alexey

"*I was cleaning myself up, wishing I had the courage to leave him. He came in and started screaming at me. I should have been fixing him something to eat. I yanked away from him and he backhanded me. I fell and hit my head on the edge of the tub. That's it. I hit my head on the tub, and my life was over.*"

"I'm so sorry."

Alexey looked at Peter. "*You're crying for me?*"

"I would have saved you. I would have protected you, but I wasn't there, Alexey."

"*All I could think was it wasn't fair. It wasn't supposed to end like this for me.*"

Peter scooted a little closer. He wished he could touch the man, do something to make him feel better. "It shouldn't have ended like that for you. You can't have Rhys's body, though."

"*Why not?*"

"Because if you take Rhys's body, then you will be no better than Demetri. It's not his time yet, Alexey. I'm sorry you died the way you did, but to take Rhys's chance of happiness is wrong."

Alexey reached for Peter, his hand going through Peter's arm.

"We don't want you to leave," Peter offered. "You just can't have Rhys's body. If you want, we can set up a marker over your grave."

Alexey lay down, hugging his knees to his chest, and looked at Peter. "*That's nice.*"

"Do you know where you're buried?"

Alexey nodded. "*In the basement behind a wall.*"

"Oh my God, you're in this basement. I need to get someone out here."

Alexey smiled. "*You don't have to. I don't mind really. I mean, if I was in the ground, no one would know where I was either.*"

181

Peter reached over, wishing he could touch the man's cheek.

"It doesn't mean we can't put a marker of some kind up." Rhys stood in the doorway.

"*I'm sorry.*" Alexey looked at him. "*I know it was wrong. I just wanted what you had so bad that I didn't realize I was becoming the person I hated.*"

"It's okay. Look, maybe we can leave your body where it is a little while longer, at least until you're ready to move it."

"*I can stay here?*" Alexey looked hopeful.

Peter looked at Rhys.

"Yeah, for a while, you can stay." Rhys sighed. "There are rules, though. No more trying to possess me. No more breaking my shit. No more slamming doors."

Alexey sat up, and wiping the tears from his face, he nodded. "*I promise not to try and kill you anymore or take over your body.*"

"Okay."

"*Can I still come to you in your dreams?*" He looked hopefully at Peter.

Peter reached out to touch Alexey's cheek, his fingers becoming numbingly cold as he made contact with the apparition. "Any time you want me, you can always see me in my dreams."

Alexey smiled, tilting his head toward Peter's hand. "*Promise?*"

"I promise, baby."

Chapter 22

"RHYS, ARE you home?" Peter called as he walked through the door.

"In the kitchen," Rhys replied.

Peter walked over to the small corner table. He pulled the flowers out of the vase and replaced them with the ones in his hand. "Here you go, Alexey."

A gentle breeze touched his skin.

"Flowers?" Rhys asked.

"I got some for you and Alexey."

"Guess who called today?"

Peter picked up the picture of Alexey they had found hidden in the attic. "Who?"

"My agent. Guess who just went to number one?"

"Oh my God!" Peter gave him a hug, spinning him around. "Do you hear that, Alexey? Rhys's game just went to number one."

There was laughter that echoed through the house.

"You know, I was thinking, if Alexey doesn't mind, I am going to turn this all into a book." Peter set Rhys back down. A slight breeze ruffled Peter's hair.

"*I would like that*" came the whispered reply.

"So what do you say we go out to eat to celebrate your success? Will you watch the house while we're gone, Alexey?"

"Thank you for the flowers." As Alexey spoke, the flowers moved in the vase.

"One happy family?" Peter asked.

"One happy family," Rhys agreed, giving him a hug.

RIDER JACOBS was raised in a small town in the corner of Kansas, where her mother instilled a love of books in her. Thanks to her mother she developed a love for all things paranormal at an early age. Her parents always encouraged her to use her imagination and write stories.

When she was eighteen she left the small farming community without a stop light and headed for the bright lights of Las Vegas. She continued to write but life kept her from actually publishing anything. After ten years in the big city, Rider decided she wanted a much slower-paced life and returned to Kansas. It was here that she met a friend who loved her stories and encouraged her to submit them.

When not writing, Rider loves to read anything she can get her hands on from the dark, taboo erotic books to the lighter Amish romance. She also has an interest in the lost art of pen-palling. Putting pen to paper and sharing the good times and the bad through the written word with friends near and far. Rider also loves to travel, and while she has been to the tourist attractions she much prefers the hidden gems off the beaten path that few know about. It is these adventures that often find their way into her books.

Rider would love to hear from you. You can follow her at:

http://riderjacobs4.wordpress.com

http://lettersforangel.wordpress.com

https://www.facebook.com/AngelRothamelAndAjKelton

Also from DREAMSPINNER PRESS

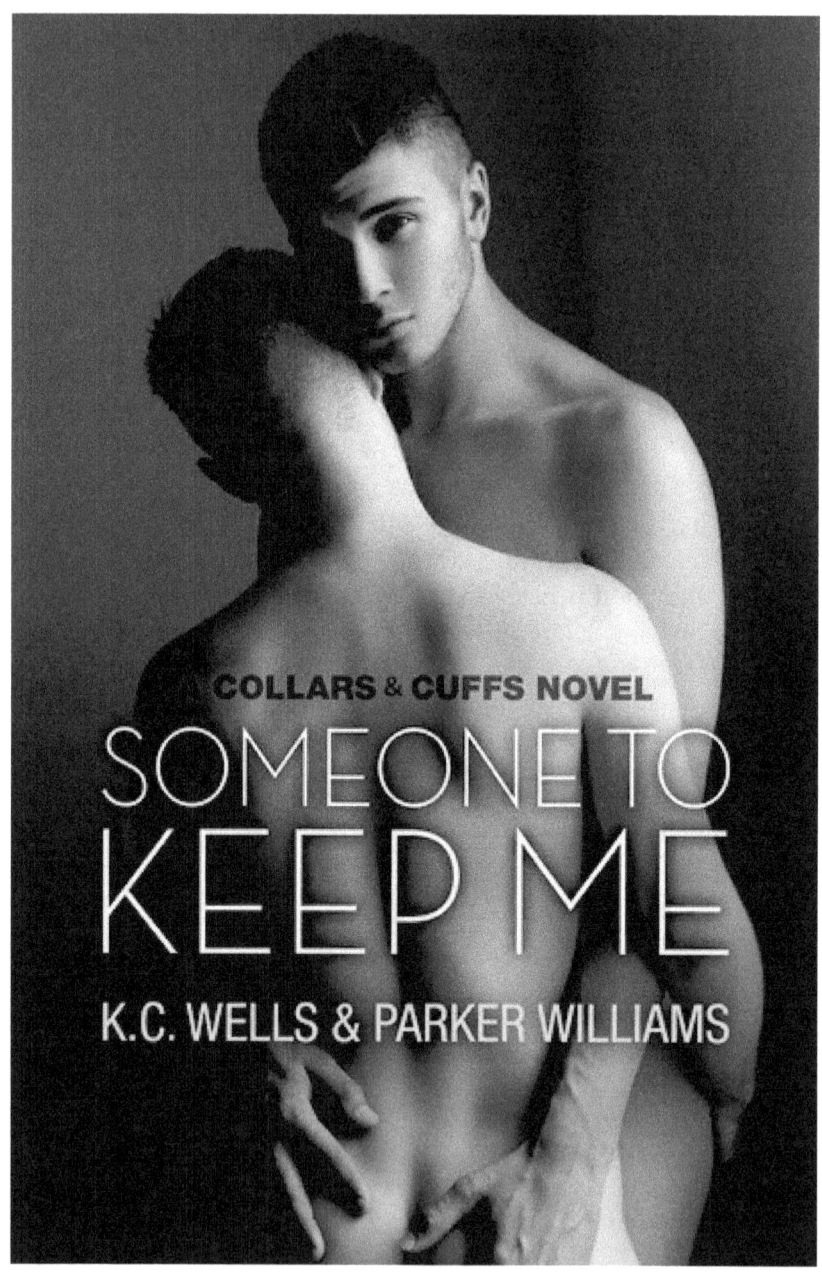

A COLLARS & CUFFS NOVEL

SOMEONE TO KEEP ME

K.C. WELLS & PARKER WILLIAMS

http://www.dreamspinnerpress.com

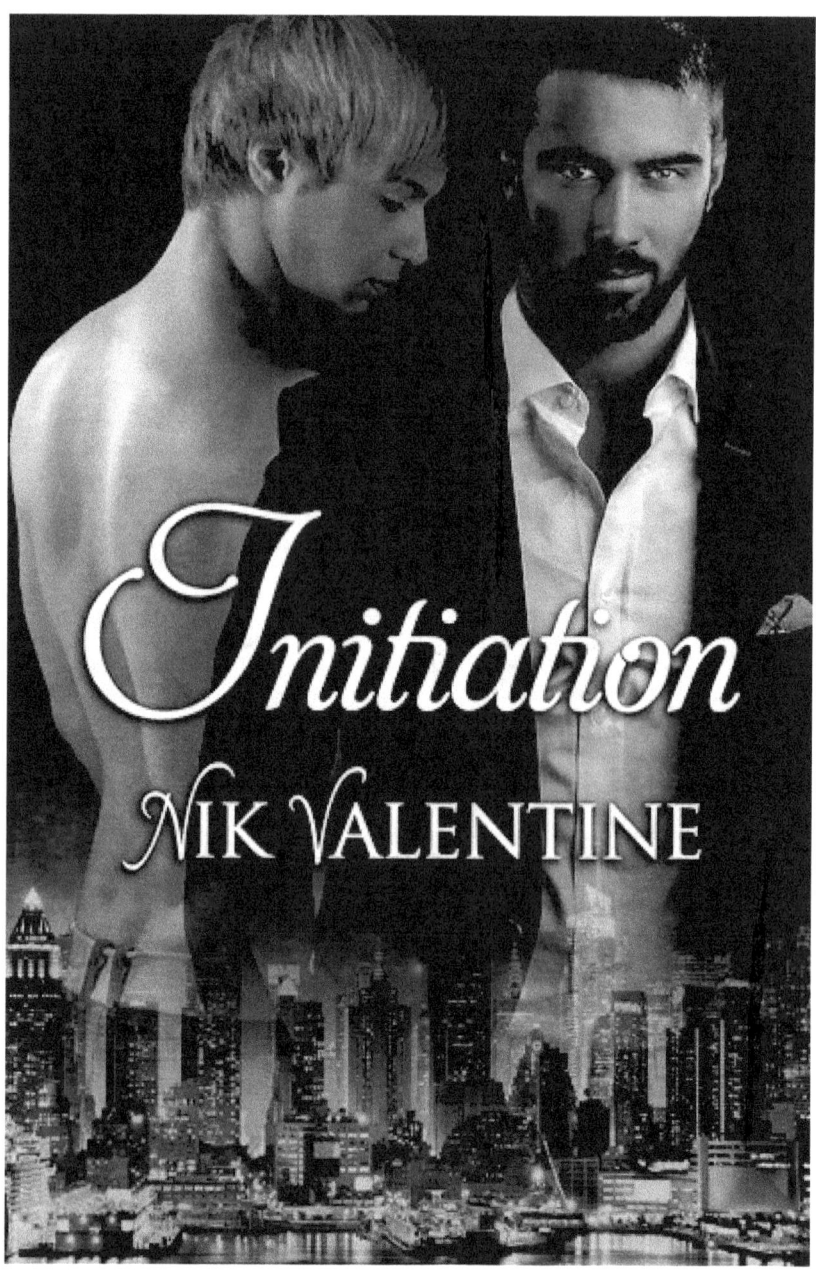

Also from DREAMSPINNER PRESS

Tia Fielding
Falling
iNTO
PLACE

http://www.dreamspinnerpress.com

Also from DREAMSPINNER PRESS

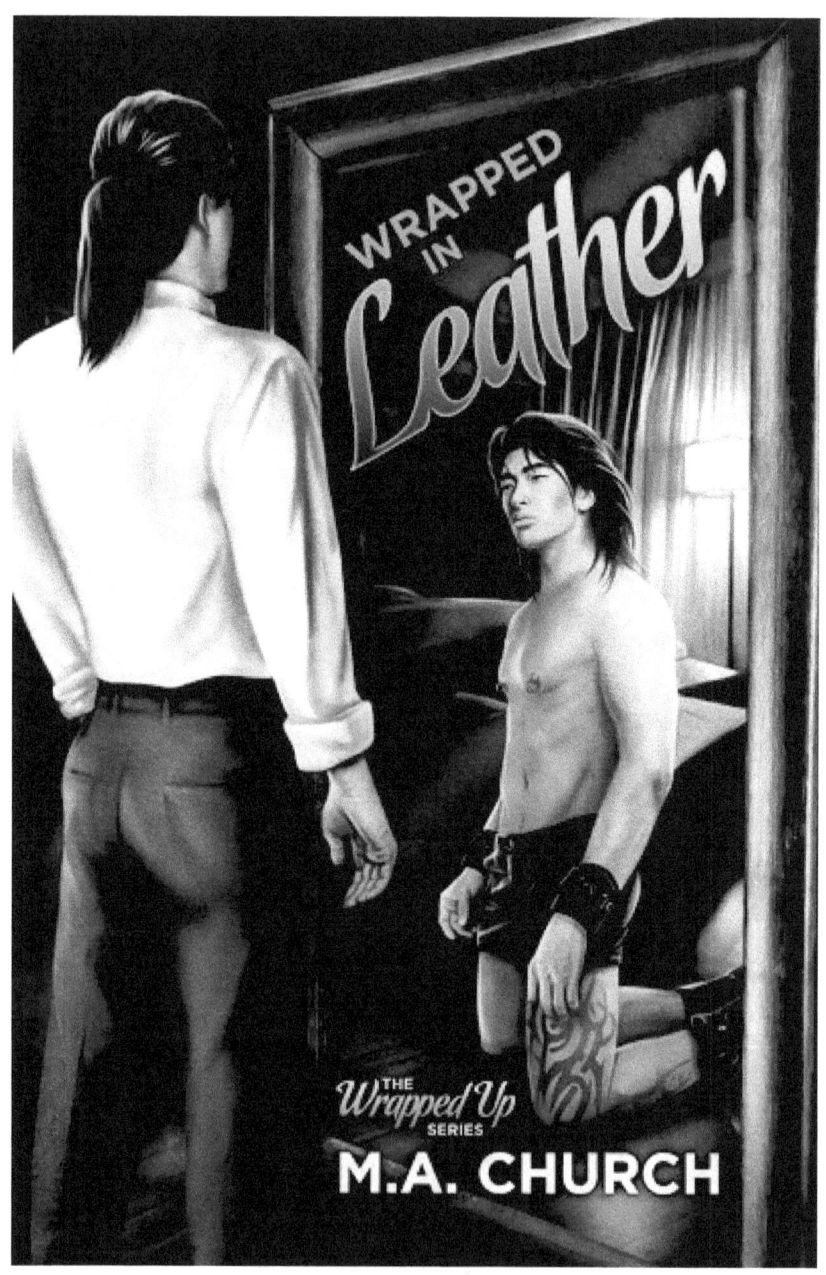

http://www.dreamspinnerpress.com

Also from DREAMSPINNER PRESS

A GUARDS OF FOLSOM NOVEL
SJD PETERSON

http://www.dreamspinnerpress.com

www.ingramcontent.com/pod-product-compliance
Lightning Source LLC
Chambersburg PA
CBHW060059260626

47160CB00005B/1719